Capone's Chaos

Capone's Chaos

By J. Lynn Lombard

J. Lynn Lombard

ROYAL BASTARDS MC SERIES
SECOND RUN

E.C. Land: *Cyclone of Chaos*
Chelle C. Craze & Eli Abbot: *Ghoul*
Scarlett Black: *Ice*
Elizabeth Knox: *Rely On Me*
J.L. Leslie: *Worth the Risk*
Deja Voss: *Lean In*
Khloe Wren: *Blaze of Honor*
Misty Walker: *Birdie's Biker*
J. Lynn Lombard: *Capone's Chaos*
Ker Dukey: *Rage*
Crimson Syn: *Scarred By Pain*
M. Merin: *Declan*
Elle Boon: *Royally F**ked*
Rae B. Lake: *Death and Paradise*
K Webster: *Copper*
Glenna Maynard: *Tempting the Biker*
K.L. Ramsey: *Whiskey Tango*
Kristine Allen: *Angel*
Nikki Landis: *Devil's Ride*
KE Osborn: *Luring Light*
CM Genovese: *Pipe Dreams*
Nicole James: *Club Princess*
Shannon Youngblood: *Leather & Chrome*
Erin Trejo: *Unbreak Me*
Winter Travers: *Six Gun*

J. Lynn Lombard

Izzy Sweet & Sean Moriarty: *Broken Ties*
Jax Hart: *Desert Rose*

Royal Bastards MC Facebook Group -
https://www.facebook.com/groups/royalbastardsmc/

Links can be found in our Website:
www.royalbastardsmc.com

Capone's Chaos

ROYAL BASTARDS CODE

PROTECT: The club and your brothers come before anything else, and must be protected at all costs. **CLUB** is **FAMILY**.

RESPECT: Earn it & Give it. Respect club law. Respect the patch. Respect your brothers. Disrespect a member and there will be hell to pay.

HONOR: Being patched in is an honor, not a right. Your colors are sacred, not to be left alone, and **NEVER** let them touch the ground.

OL' LADIES: Never disrespect a member's or brother's Ol'Lady. **PERIOD.**

CHURCH is **MANDATORY.**

LOYALTY: Takes precedence over all, including well-being.

HONESTY: Never **LIE, CHEAT,** or **STEAL** from another member or the club.

TERRITORY: You are to respect your brother's property and follow their Chapter's club rules.

TRUST: Years to earn it...seconds to lose it.

NEVER RIDE OFF: Brothers do not abandon their family.

J. Lynn Lombard

Capone's Chaos

WARNING

Welcome to the Royal Bastards world. If blood, guts, gore, and a world full of dark, one-percenters isn't your forte, then kindly turn around and leave. What you're about to read isn't for everyone. If you have sexual triggers, then this isn't for you. The Royal Bastard authors don't write sunshine and roses. We write dark, gritty books that will test your limits and leave you breathless.

If you're still here, welcome to our world…

J. Lynn Lombard

Capone's Chaos
Royal Bastards MC Los Angeles book 2
By J. Lynn Lombard

A Man In Control. A Lost Soul. One Last Chance.

Capone

As President of the Royal Bastards MC, Los Angeles Chapter, I have enemies everywhere. They'll use anything and anyone to exploit me. Regardless, only one person has ever brought me to my knees. Danyella.
My Belle.
Her emerald green eyes captured my soul the moment we looked at each other. I constantly watch her and the light in her eyes is fading. Her laughter and smiles all but gone. I realize that my enemies have found my kryptonite. She's become their pawn, and there's only one way to get her back.
Revenge.

Danyella

The first time I heard his deep, raspy voice, it sent chills down my spine. He called me, "My Belle." If only he knew how much those two words crushed me. Derek is lethal. He's ruthless and he can never know what I've done to protect his Club and my heart. The struggle to climb out of the hole I buried myself in is real. I've been

Capone's Chaos

slowly sinking into the shadows, trying to find a way into the light again, but all I see is darkness all around me with no way out.

J. Lynn Lombard

Prologue

Capone

5 years ago

"Get this piece of shit out of here." I kick Chains' limp, bloody body as I pass, growling at the shaking prospect. He needs to grow a set of balls if he wants to make it in the Royal Bastards MC.

I knew this would happen soon. Chains has been losing the respect of this club for the past few years. Only a few brothers stood by him when he came at me tonight. I saw what he was doing and how he was destroying the club and had to make a decision. Let him continue to destroy our livelihood or take it from him. So, I took it from him.

A few nights ago, he went after my little sister, Monica. By the time Blayze and I got to him, she had bruises on her arms and hips and I knew I had to send her away. Before she left, our mother was spiraling down a destructive path. After Monica, Blayze and I got her hidden away from Chains, she confessed her darkest secret. It crushed me knowing she's been lying to me my whole life, but I get it.

Capone's Chaos

Chains is an egotistical asshole and if he found out what my mom did, he would've killed her and then me. So, I put a plan into action and here we are. Destruction and chaos surrounding me.

Torch and Trigger have Chains' VP, Shooter, strung up by his wrists. His feet barely touching the ground. They're the only two out of the old Royal Bastards to fight us on the change. The rest either fell in line or left. And those who left are dead to me. I won't hesitate to kill them if they step foot into my clubhouse.

"Wake his fucking ass up," I growl at Torch. Torch curls his upper lip and dumps a bucket of ice-cold water on Shooter. Shooter spits and sputters, cursing is under his breath.

"What's that old fucker? You got something to say?" My fingers dig into the soft flesh of Shooter's jawbone and squeeze. I can feel his bones rub together under my grip. "Do you have a problem?"

"You're going to fucking pay for this, Capone." Shooter bows his body, trying to pull away from my death grip. I don't give him an inch.

"No, cock sucker, you're going to pay for trying to harm my sister and destroy my club." I deliver a deadly blow to his ribs, feeling them crack under the pressure. Shooter grunts in pain bringing satisfaction to my dark soul. I hit him again and again until he stops struggling and my arms are heavy.

J. Lynn Lombard

"Prez, he isn't breathing anymore." Blayze, my VP, grips my shoulder halting my next blow. I look into Shooter's lifeless eyes staring back at me and satisfaction burns through my body.

"Take Chains to the desert and leave him there. I don't give a fuck if he lives or not." I snap at the prospect who still hasn't moved. "Now!" The prospect jumps and grabs an unconscious Chains by his armpits, dragging him out of the room. I turn toward Torch and Trigger. "Get this piece of shit out of here and get rid of his body."

Torch hits a button and the pulley system we have in place drops Shooter's lifeless body onto the concrete floor with a thud. My brothers have this under control, now it's time to get back to the raging party going on upstairs in my Clubhouse.

I climb the wooden stairs of the basement and make my way to the bar. Red, the Secretary for Royal Bastards, and his prospect, Bones, are slinging drinks tonight. Red spots me and fills up a glass of whiskey, sliding it down to the end of the bar. I grip it with a bloody fist and pound the drink back. The burn of whiskey going down my throat and into my stomach settles the adrenaline flowing through my veins. Now, it's time to find a tight pussy to get lost in.

My eyes scour the room looking for a patch whore to relieve this pent-up aggression on. They fall upon a blonde-haired beauty dancing, definitely not a patch whore. A small, tight black dress hugs her

Capone's Chaos

curves, her hips are swaying seductively to the beat of the music. Everything else fades away as she captivates me as no other has done before. She opens her eyes and familiar green ones stare back at me. I'm lost in her tranquil gaze that sees past the rage, past the hate, past the anger and into the depths of my dark soul.

I release a low growl and stand up. Stalking my prey, I saunter toward the warm body of my Belle. She's mine and doesn't even realize it yet. My fingers dig into her swaying hips, my head lowers to smell her intoxicating scent. Danyella sways her hips seductively to the beat of some chick singing about talking bodies. My hands roam up her hips, brush past her tits and grips the sides of her face. She spins around and nips at my fingertips that are gently cupping her face. My forehead resting against Danyella's, I breathe her in. My body is trembling with need. Sparks fly from my fingertips in her mouth, up to my arm and straight to my aching cock begging for release.

"Hey, Prez, you're needed in Church." Torch interrupts us, bursting the seductive bubble Danyella and I are wrapped in.

I breathe harshly through my nose and release her from my grip. A low groan rips from my throat, "This fucking better be important." I pin Torch with a deadly glare.

"It is." Torch's dark eyes hold nothing back. They're all worried about the info I found out through my mother.

Turning my attention back to Danyella, who's watching us cautiously, "I have to go. Don't go anywhere."

Her nostrils flare and her green eyes flame with anger, "I'm not one of your patch whores, Capone." Danyella spits out. "If you want me, you'll have to find me." She spins on her heels, her long blonde hair whipping as she goes and takes off through the clubhouse. Fuck my life.

If I would've known that was the last time the two of us would be that close, I would've told Torch to fuck off and Church could wait. But I didn't and chaos ensued for many years after.

Capone's Chaos

Chapter 1

Capone 16 years old

"Get the fuck over here boy." My father, Chains, the President of Royal Bastards, bellows across the clubhouse. He's constantly shouting at me and it sets my teeth on edge. I can't stand the motherfucker and the day he is taken down will be the happiest day of my life. We look and act nothing alike. Chains is short and stout, his dark hair is peppered with grey. He's an asshole to everyone, including his own son. We're completely opposite as I'm tall and muscled with my shiny black hair. I can't stand him and whenever he bellows at me, I ignore him for as long as I can.

"Capone, now!" That's my cue. Shit will hit the fan if I don't go over there. I slide off the barstool and make my way over to Chains sitting at a round table with a patch whore on his lap while my mother looks on like she doesn't care. Some other brothers are sitting around the table and they stare at me with smirks on their faces I want to wipe off with my fist. My cut after two years of paying my dues is now a Royal Bastards instead of a prospect.

J. Lynn Lombard

"Can I help you with something?" I address the whole table. All four of them smirk, waiting for Chains' order.

"You will address me as Prez when you speak, boy." The psychotic gleam in his dark eyes is daring me to step out of line. I've played this game with him for years. Taking the brunt of his wrath away from my sister, Monica.

My teeth grind together before I speak. "What do you need, Prez?" The word vomit is threatening to make its way up my throat. I tap it down before I say something that will cause pain on my mother and sister. Oh yeah, Chains knows the way to get me to comply is to go after my mother and sister. He realized when I turned fifteen, he couldn't touch me anymore. Now, he goes after the weaker sex and it keeps me compliant. But I'm biding my time, waiting for the right moment to strike and hit him where it hurts. His Presidency.

"We have a couple of guests coming in today. You need to make sure their room is ready." Chains commands.

"Isn't that the patch whores' job?" I raise an eyebrow at the one named Bambi sitting on his lap, draping her body around him.

"Well, as you can see, they're all busy." He sniffs the side of her neck and she giggles setting my teeth on edge. "You got a problem, boy?" The way he

Capone's Chaos

says the word boy has the hair on the back of my neck stand on edge.

"No problem, Prez." I spit the word out like it's a bad taste in my mouth. When I really want to send my fist into his face, shoving his teeth down his throat. Loyalty to the Royal Bastards is what stops me from following through. My time will come.

"Good. Now get the shit ready. An old member's son and his sister will be here in less than an hour." Chains goes back to nuzzling the patch whore on her neck, making her squirm and giggle.

I turn on the heel of my boots and swear to the motherfucking biker Gods, when I end him, this shit will not be happening in my club. Not while his wife, my mother, is sitting in the next room. I will not tolerate the disrespect for women that Chains and his men have.

I approach my mother, her tiny body sitting on the couch, staring off into space. I rest my hand on her shoulder, startling her. She looks up at me with her brown eyes, blinking a few times. Her Mexican heritage is strong in her features.

"Will you come help me, Mom?" I ask, needing to get her away from the scene unfolding behind us. I know it'll be a matter of time before Chains has Bambi on her knees while he fucks her mouth and my mother doesn't need to be subjected to that.

J. Lynn Lombard

She nods her head and rises from the couch. Once we're out of earshot, I ask the question that has been burning in my head for the last few months. Ever since Chains stopped hiding the fact that he's fucking patch whores and does it in front of my mother.

"Why do you let him do this to you?"

"It doesn't matter." She answers.

"Yes, it does. He's disrespecting you and everything we stand for when he plays with his whore in front of you." My voice shakes with anger.

My mom grabs some sheets out of a closet and enters an extra room. I follow behind, waiting for some kind of answer. Inside the room are two beds, two dressers, a stand next to each bed, a closet and a bathroom. She walks over to one of the beds and starts putting the fitted sheet on. I help, waiting for her to tell me what is going on.

She releases a deep sigh, her brown eyes shiny with tears, "Derek, this is the life I chose. I can't change it no matter how bad I want to. There are things no one knows about and if certain people find out, it will be bad. Very bad."

"Mom, I want to help you. I want to take this pain away. But I can't if you don't tell me what it is." I rest my hand on her shoulder and she leans into me.

"I know, Derek. But I can't."

Capone's Chaos

"Please, mom. This is killing you. You can't keep living like this."

She looks around the room, her eyes darting in every direction. She looks up at me with a sad smile on her face. "Derek, you're such a good kid. Don't let him change you." Her tiny hand cups the side of my face, warm and inviting. "The decisions I made will affect you and your sister." She lowers her voice to a whisper, "There are ears everywhere. If he finds out, we're both dead. So, be careful because I think he already knows."

"Knows? Knows what?"

"I've said too much. Come on, let's finish this up before he comes looking for us." She can't and won't ever say Chains' name.

We finish making the beds and air the room out. Mom disappears down the hallway, probably toward her room. She doesn't share one with Chains anymore and honestly, I don't blame her. My mind is still reeling from our cryptic conversation when my feet carry me into the commons room.

Chains is no longer sitting at the round table with Shooter, his V.P. and a few other brothers. I look around for him but he's nowhere in sight. Thank fuck he took the whore out of the room to fuck her. Moans and giggles can be heard coming from his closed office door behind the commons room. A slap and a moan followed by a grunt pierce the quiet room. I walk to the table, staring at his loyal members.

"Does listening to him beat and fuck a whore get your dicks up?" I turn up the music until I can't hear them anymore and stomp out of the room toward the garage before I see red and beat every one of them with their own limp dicks. Another thing to add to my list to take them down when the time comes.

The alarm buzzes telling me we have a visitor at the front gates. I open the garage door and see an older matte black motorcycle idling in front of the gates, waiting to be let in. Two people are on it, one is a man and the other is a woman. The woman is wearing a backpack and both have on full-face helmets. Liquid talks to them for a moment and lets them in. The motorcycle growls when it turns and heads toward me. I step out of the doorway and let them inside the garage. The rider parks the bike, shuts it off and motions for the passenger to climb off. She swings her leg over, slides the backpack off and sets it on the floor. The driver climbs off and removes his helmet. His blonde hair is shaggy in the front, short in the back. He's about my size with sleeve tattoos filling up both arms. He turns to help the girl with her helmet before hanging them both on the handlebars of his bike.

The girl shakes her long blonde hair before turning toward me. My heart picks up a rapid beat in my chest. She's the most beautiful girl I've ever seen,

Capone's Chaos

with piercing green eyes staring at me. I'm speechless.

"Welcome to the Royal Bastards," Chains bellows down the hallway before stepping into the garage. His hair is disheveled and he's zipping his pants with a satisfied smirk on his face I want to wipe off. He's leering at the girl, who can't be older than fifteen, with a predator gleam in his black eyes. Rage consumes every pour in my body and my hands shake. "Make yourselves at home."

The guy moves in front of the girl with a stiff posture, blocking her from Chains' view. "Names Blayze and this is my sister Danyella." Blayze crosses his arms over his chest, daring anyone to do something to his sister.

"Your father was a great member of this Club, God rest his soul. Hopefully, you will be too. Blayze and Danyella, come on inside. It appears my son has lost his manners along with his tongue." Chains reprimands me while plastering on a fake smile. He leads the way into the commons room with Blayze and Danyella behind him and me bringing up the rear.

Bambi is back, sitting at the table with fresh red marks around her neck, laughing with Shooter. He's leaning in close and grabs her tit. She squeals and moans. Chains leaves us standing in the middle of the room and goes back over to the table. Bambi stands up and sits on Chains' lap when he sits back down. It turns my stomach the way they pass off the women in the club. Thank fuck they haven't turned my sister into a whore like the rest of them. Doesn't mean they won't try with Danyella. Her fresh, young look will turn her into prey to these fuckers if I don't do something quick.

I step up next to both Blayze and Danyella crossing my arms over my chest. The need to protect her flows strongly through my blood. I'm not sure what it is about her, but I'll do everything I can to make sure no harm comes to either of them. "Follow me and I'll show you to your room."

Danyella reaches to pick up the backpack she and I grab it at the same time. Our fingers brush and a storm starts low in my belly. I lift my eyes to hers and she's staring at me open-mouthed. She felt that spark too. I grab her bag and the three of us walk down the hallway into their room.

"It's temporary right now, but I figured you'd want to bunk together. It'd be the safer choice for the time being." I'm cryptic but if Blayze is prospecting for Royal Bastards, he should know what I mean by it.

A light knock on the door draws our attention, "Hey, Capone. Do you have a minute?" My sister Monica stands in the doorway fidgeting with the hem of her shirt. She's only fourteen but has seen so many things no teenager should see.

Capone's Chaos

"Give me a minute and I'll be right there." Her brown eyes look relieved until they land on Blayze, then her cheeks turn a shade of pink. I sigh, this girl will be the death of me, I swear. "Monica, this is Blayze and his sister Danyella. Blayze and Danyella, my little sister, Monica." I gesture between the three of them.

"Hi," Monica plays shy. This girl is anything but shy. She has a mouth like a sailor and can hold her own against anyone. Shy is not in her vocabulary. That's the way our mother raised her. To be strong and resilient toward everything and everyone. Raising an eyebrow, I give her a questioning look.

"I'll be back in a little bit to show you around." I look at Danyella keeping my voice as soft as possible so I don't scare her. "Don't wander around alone, it's not safe right now." I look at Blayze and he nods his head so I continue. I don't know how much she understands the club life but I'm going to give her a quick, hard lesson. The need to touch her again overpowers me and I rest a palm on her shoulder gently. Sparks shoot through my fingertips, down my stomach and straight to my groin. "I don't want to scare you, but those men at that table, aren't good people. For your safety and your brother's sanity, don't wander around alone. If you want to go somewhere, get me, Blayze or Monica."

Danyella stares up at me with her big green eyes full of trust and understanding. "I've been around MC's before. I know what they're like and how to handle it but thank you for keeping me safe." It's the first words she's said since they got here and her quiet voice is like an angel singing. I could sit and listen to her talk all day long. She smiles at me and it does something to my soul. Something I can't explain and don't want to.

Who would've thought this moment would change the course of my life? I never would've thought a girl I just met would look at me like I hung the moon and the stars and everything I do and strive for from this point forward is centered around her. I will protect her with my life and do everything I can to make sure she's safe and cherished. I will stake my claim on her and no one will touch her.

Capone's Chaos

Chapter 2

Capone Present

My little sister married. Who the fuck would have thought her and Blayze would tie the knot so quickly? I should've seen it coming though. The way those two would eye fuck each other when they thought no one was watching. Or the way Blayze had to touch her, even just passing by. Then after what Steam from Savage Saints, Detroit, did to her and the way we found her, Blayze wouldn't let Monica leave his side. He fought through hell to get her and keep her by his side. Which is why tonight, we're celebrating the first member of Royal Bastards to be tied down to one woman forever.

Blayze and Monica's wedding. We've all did horrible things to protect Monica. Things we wouldn't change, even if asked. That's what makes us the elite one-percenters. We only follow the Royal Bastards rules, which are proudly displayed above the bar. It's the first thing someone sees when they enter our Clubhouse.

J. Lynn Lombard

PROTECT: The club and your brothers come before anything else, and must be protected at all costs. **CLUB** is **FAMILY**.

RESPECT: Earn it & Give it. Respect club law. Respect the patch. Respect your brothers. Disrespect a member and there will be hell to pay.

HONOR: Being patched in is an honor, not a right. Your colors are sacred, not to be left alone, and **NEVER** let them touch the ground.

OL' LADIES: Never disrespect a member's or brother's Ol'Lady. **PERIOD.**

CHURCH is **MANDATORY.**

LOYALTY: Takes precedence over all, including well-being.

HONESTY: Never **LIE, CHEAT,** or **STEAL** from another member or the club.

TERRITORY: You are to respect your brother's property and follow their Chapter's club rules.

TRUST: Years to earn it...seconds to lose it.

NEVER RIDE OFF: Brothers do not abandon their family.

Anyone who doesn't follow these sacred rules will be punished. We, the Royal Bastards, are the judge, jury and executioners.

Whistling and pounding draw me out of my mind and my dark eyes land on my Belle. She's

Capone's Chaos

swaying her hips to the beat of a song wearing a silk grey bridesmaid dress that hugs her curves. My eyes travel from the tips of her painted toes, up her long lean legs, to the swell of her tits, up her neck until they land on her face. Her eyes are open and she's watching me, watch her. It's the sexiest thing I've seen in my life. Her green eyes are hooded with desire. My cock aches to belong to only her. My lips crave her plump ones.

I don't know what it is about Danyella that I'm attracted to. I don't know why my body knows where she is at any given time. I don't know how she has this power over me. Some people believe in insta-love, but I don't. I've known Danyella since she and Blayze came to the Royal Bastards and he prospected for us. They were sixteen and fifteen. The first time I laid eyes on her, I staked my claim on her to any brother who had other ideas. She didn't know I did it and no one touched her or told her. All these years later, my claim still stands.

After she was kidnapped last year, I totally lost my head. Patch whores came and went, trying to please me to take the edge off, but none of them could do it. None of them could come even close and it frustrated me. All my brothers thought I was getting action every night or day but little did they know, my dick wouldn't stand unless thoughts of my Belle were in my head. None of the patch whores said a word. If they did, they were gone forever.

J. Lynn Lombard

Every day I was angry and bitter, lashing out at everyone, even my own brothers. No one understood why and I didn't tell them. I'd grunt or growl making those six months she was taken unbearable for everyone. Keeping my emotions inside almost killed me. Almost lost my Prez spot. I was toxic to everyone around me and I couldn't change it. No matter how hard I tried to shove my feelings for Danyella away, they wouldn't go.

Then, when Blayze and Monica found Daisy in Monica's porn studio being raped by J.J., everything came into the light. We finally got a lead and we found my Belle, beaten and raped. The shit she lived through traumatized her. She watched other women being taken and forced to fuck against their wills. The Bloody Scorpions never touched my Belle in that way. If they did, I would have killed them all, then brought them back from the dead and murdered them all over again. But Dred did and she got her bittersweet revenge. Now, instead of being scared of my touch, she's practically begging me from across the dance floor.

My feet move across the room onto the dance floor and I pull Danyella's sexy body against mine. She grinds her hips, moving her ass into my aching cock and sways to the beat of the music pumping through the speakers. Everything and everyone fades away as I inhale her sweet scent and let her move against me, using my body the way she needs to. I crave her touch, her flavor on my tongue. Hot and heavy, sexual tension radiates between us as we get lost in each other. Each dip of her hips sends a shock to my heart. Each breath Danyella expels washes over me, captivating my attention.

She turns around so we're chest to chest. My heart is galloping hard ready to explode out of my chest. I lick my dry lips and her green eyes drift down, her lashes flutter against her skin. She peeks up at me through her thick lashes and that's my undoing. My lips crash down onto hers capturing them in one swoop. Danyella wraps her arms around my neck, pulling me closer to her and releases a moan from the back of her throat. She opens her mouth, sucking my tongue into her hot, wet cavern. I wrap my arms around her waist pulling her tight against me. I break the kiss and rest my forehead against hers, breathing heavily. Enjoying her taste on my tongue, I dive back in and kiss her again.

We get carried away and before my brain catches up with my aching dick, Danyella and I are in a dark corner, locked in each other's embrace, our lips devouring each other. Her hot breath fanning over my heated skin, moans and whimpers escaping her delicate throat. She's straddling me, her sweet pussy grinding against my stiff cock begging for release. Lost in this lust-filled haze, I should stop her, but I can't deny her anything she needs, anything she wants. If she needs to use me to erase the pain haunting her, I'll gladly offer up my body. Shouts and catcalls pull me out of my lust induced haze, slamming me back to reality.

J. Lynn Lombard

"Belle, wait," I groan against her heated skin. I stop Danyella from freeing my cock and making a big mistake. My body is screaming at me to continue while my mind is telling me no. I can't defile her beautiful soul with the darkness I carry with me. No matter how bad I want too.

Danyella's face falls and tears gleam in her eyes. "I thought we were on the same page, Derek." My name rolling off her tongue has my heart slamming hard against my chest. I want to say fuck it. I want to give in to the temptation right in front of me, but I can't. Not with all this baggage following me around.

"I'm no good for you, Belle. I can't drag your beauty down into my darkness." I look in her eyes and her lips tremble. I want to claim those lips and kiss away the pain I've caused, but now that I'm slammed back into reality, I can't. She deserves better than I can give her.

Danyella climbs off my lap and walks away without another word. She's doesn't look back and doesn't stop. She disappears out of my sight and that's the last time she gives me any attention.

Capone's Chaos

Chapter 3

Capone

A phone ringing in the distance pulls me awake and I groan, rolling over. My head is pounding hard against my skull and my mouth is drier than the Sahara Desert. After Danyella walked away from me last night heartbroken and angry, I found myself wallowing in a bottle of Whiskey. I know it's all my fault I put that hurt in her heart, but it's for the best. I can't give in to my weakness, not while shit's hitting the fan that no one knows about yet. My phone rings again and I slap my hand around the nightstand looking for it without opening my eyes.

"Capone," I grunt answering my phone.

"Capone, Jameson. I need you to fly to NOLA asap. Bring Blayze. We have unfinished business." Jameson is the National Charter Prez. When he calls, you jump.

I sit up in bed and excitement pounds through my veins, "Does this mean what I think it does?"

J. Lynn Lombard

"You bet your ass it does. Get here today." Jameson hangs up on me and I climb out of bed. My skull still feels like it's been fucked by little gnomes, but the adrenaline pounding through my veins subsides the hangover I should feel.

I toss my phone on the nightstand and light up a cigarette. Inhaling the nicotine deep into my lungs, I open the mini-fridge and grab a water. Downing it in two gulps, I feel better but I need a shower and a pot of coffee to curb this hangover from hell. I text Blayze to warn his ass to meet me in the kitchen in twenty. I don't want or need to hear him and my sister fucking like rabbits. Shitty timing for them since they just got married yesterday, but when the club calls, we go, no matter what we're doing or who's pussy were balls deep in.

I stub out my smoke and stumble into the bathroom. After taking a piss, I start the shower letting the steam fill the room. I step inside and my mind brings up an image of Danyella dancing in her grey dress last night. The way the fabric hugged her lavishing curves. The way her hands roamed over my chest and tugged my hair when she was straddling me in the corner. Her hot breath panting in my ear while my palms gripped her hips tight. The way she moved against me releasing little whimpers from the back of her throat and my cock is rock solid. I grab my shaft at the base and pull upward. I imagine her on her knees looking up at me through her lashes while she takes my length into her mouth until the head hits the back of her throat. I stroke my cock at a fast

Capone's Chaos

pace, imaging it's her plump lips wrapped around my cock, sucking hard. A growl rips from my throat as tingles work their way down my spine and my cock grows harder. She's sucking me hard while playing with her tits moaning around my cock filling her mouth and throat. I come so hard, panting and my knees buckle from relief.

I'm a selfish, dirty bastard but right now, I really don't give a fuck. I messed up last night pushing her away. I never should've let her go, no matter what my mind thinks. I finish my shower, somewhat sated. I'll never be fully satisfied with my own hand until I have her in my bed and in my life. I dry off and throw on a pair of blue jeans, a black tee with the Royal Bastards logo, socks and my riding boots. I slide on my cut, grab my wallet and keys and leave the comfort of my bedroom masking my face into the heartless bastard everyone's accustomed to.

My headache makes a strong reappearance as I walk down the quiet hallway. Coffee, I need a strong gallon of coffee to get these little fuckers to stop drilling inside my head. I pass a few patch whores sprawled out on the couches naked as the day their face came through their mother's cunt and walk into the kitchen. My steps falter and my mouth turns dry. At the stove is my Belle wearing tiny sleep shorts, a tank top and her sexy feet are bare with pink polish on each nail. She's swaying her hips to a beat only she can hear while scrambling eggs. I watch from the doorway like a creeper, not giving a fuck. Turning around to plate the food on the marble countertop, I see Belle has earphones in and doesn't look up. I know she knows I'm here. The rapid rising and falling of her chest and the pink flush on her cheeks gives her away. I saunter into the kitchen and sit on the stool directly in front of her. Danyella doesn't even look at me when she turns the stove off and walks away. If it were anyone else, they'd be out on their ass, but I get why she's so mad at me. I hurt her badly and for once in my life, I don't know how to fix it.

My phone rings at the same time Blayze and Monica come stumbling into the kitchen with their hands all over each other giggling. It's Scorch, the Prez from the Elizabeth City, NC Chapter. I swipe the green button to answer. "This better be good, Scorch. I'm in the middle of something," I snap. Monica giggles while Blayze manhandles her. I turn my back on them.

"I can tell," Scorch chuckles. "Look, wanted to see if you can do us a favor."

My interest is peaked. I'm all the way across the country, not sure what I can help with. "What kind of favor you asking for?"

"One where you get Torch to cause some fireworks down in Mexico out at the Alcazar's." Scorch is dead serious about this. He gives me a rundown on what's going on out there and their plan. The more he talks, the more I'm interested. Alcazar is causing a lot of problems for my brothers and we

Capone's Chaos

have some unfinished business down in Mexico anyways. Kill two birds with one stone.

"I'm sure it can be arranged, when do you need it done?" I ask.

"Soon as possible."

"We're heading to NOLA right now, but when we get back, I can make it happen." The sheer thrill in my voice is unmistakable. It's been a while since Torch blew shit up.

"Thanks, brother," Scorch mutters before we hang up.

I turn to Blayze watching me and I shake my head. I'll fill him in later, not in front of his wife. I plate some eggs and bacon and grab a cup of coffee. I shovel a fork full of food into my mouth.

"Babe, want something to eat?" Monica asks Blayze.

"You know what I want to eat and it's not food, Bug." The deep growl of Blayze's voice sends Monica into a lust-filled haze and my teeth on edge.

"Really you two? I get you just got married but I'm trying to fucking eat here." I bark.

"C'mon big bro. What or should I ask who's got your panties in a bunch?" Monica asks.

"Nothing," I grumble around a mouth full of delicious eggs.

J. Lynn Lombard

"Bullshit," Danyella appears at the doorway of the kitchen glaring at me. "Why don't you ask him what happened last night."

I swallow hard. My appetite has suddenly vanished when three sets of eyes land on me. I pick up my plate with a scowl on my face, "We're leaving in fifteen. Be ready." I toss my plate into the sink not giving a fuck if it breaks and stomps out of the room. I don't need her fucking glare pointed at me. I already know I fucked up. I don't need reminders on it.

I walk out the back door needing some air and light up a smoke. The sun is high in the sky, warming my face as soon as I step outside. L.A. weather is beautiful any time of year. Which is why living here is so peaceful. The salty air from the sea burns my lungs, the heat from the sun warms my skin.

The Royal Bastards clubhouse sits on a dirt road away from houses and cars. We don't have a normal clubhouse. You must follow the road that leads to a long driveway and ride up to a chain-link fence surrounding a huge cement building that used to be a warehouse at one time but now belongs to the Royal Bastards MC. There's a guard shack to the left in front of the fence unmanned. After Samantha, the Club Bitch, infiltrated our security when she and the Bloody Scorpions kidnapped Monica, we tightened our defense. The only way in or out of this place is through the rolling gates. We set security cameras up in every corner of the building and the

Capone's Chaos

blind spot along the fence moving with us on motion sensors. You enter and turn to the left of the gates, past the parking lot and roll up to the white garage doors. Each of us have a button on our bikes and the door rolls up for us to enter. The fluorescent lights turn on the motion sensors detecting our movements.

A long corridor leads deep into the clubhouse. In the commons room to the left are the pool tables and dartboards. To the right are a few couches and chairs set up in front of a seventy-inch-widescreen TV.

To the back of the commons room is the bar. Behind the bar is our club logo etched in a mirrored glass along with the Royal Bastards club rules. Twenty-six Chapters range from the east coast starting in Boston, MA; NYC; Baltimore, MD, North Carolina, all the way south to Tampa and Miami, FL then across the US through Georgia, Mississippi, Louisiana, Tennessee, Kentucky, Missouri, West Virginia, Michigan, Colorado, Nebraska, Texas, to the west coast in Arizona, California, Nevada and Alaska. Twenty-six Chapters all over the US and we're expanding overseas too. If any one of them needs anything, we drop what we're doing and go in a heartbeat. Loyalty to the Club goes before everything else. It doesn't matter if you're balls deep in your Ol' Lady on your honeymoon in Cabo. If a Chapter needs help, you are there with no hesitation.

J. Lynn Lombard

"Hey, Prez." Torch approaches me with cautious steps out back.

I glare at him and inhale the nicotine deep into my lungs. "Blayze and I have to leave for a few days. Bear will be in charge. Get with him and make sure everything is still set up for the meets and fights. We should be back in three, maybe four days tops." Clean money for our Club filters through the MMA fighting ring, a few bars, a porn studio and a mechanic shop. We run our illegal dealings with guns and weed, never any hard stuff, and taking care of known criminals without a trace.

"Is everything OK?" Torch who's known not to give a fuck except blowing things up and enforcing our rules asking this question tells me I'm not doing a good enough job of hiding my feelings.

"Yeah, it's all good, brother." I slap him on the back and head into the clubhouse. "I'll have a job for you when we get back, brother. Be ready to let off some fireworks south of the border." I call out over my shoulder. I don't have to see his face to know he's smiling from ear to ear. I walk into my room and pack a bag. Heading out to the garage, I'm on my bike waiting for Blayze. Not long after, he shows up with Monica tucked under his arm. A twinge of jealousy burns my chest watching the two of them. Blayze kisses Monica and then throws his helmet on and mounts his bike. She leans in and gives him another kiss before we take off. Riding into the sun and toward LAX, I relax a little. Images of a feisty blonde

Capone's Chaos

pop into my head and I know I have to figure out a way to make Danyella officially mine. Once I get this business with Jameson in NOLA taken care of, I will fix what's broken between us.

J. Lynn Lombard

Chapter 4

Danyella

As the deep rumbles of Derek and Xander's bikes fade into the distance, I release a deep sigh and head back into the clubhouse. A place that's been home for Blayze and me for the last several years. I wanted to go to Capone, run my fingers through his dark hair, give him a goodbye kiss and wish him luck on his trip, but I don't have the right to do that. Not now and probably not ever. After the way he pushed me away last night, it's clear he isn't interested in me that way. Probably never will be. After all the baggage I carry with the kidnapping and assault, no one would want my fucked-up head anyways.

Bloody Scorpions might not have touched me physically, but they did some mental damage. The one who did rape and beat me is now dead by my hands. I want control back of my life. I might never be the way I once was, but I need to find a way to overcome the things stopping me and become a better woman. A woman who can push aside her own feelings for the man she craves. A woman who

Capone's Chaos

can handle the president of a motorcycle club and all the things that come with it.

My phone vibrates in my pocket and a sense of dread washes over me. I ignore it like I have for the last several months. I don't know how long I can continue to ignore it, but I'm going to for as long as I can. I can't bring myself to accept the fact I have another secret I'm hiding from the whole club and I'm afraid when they find out, I'll be disowned and out on my ass faster than I can breathe.

I'm sick and tired of being weak. I'm done being pushed around by men who have no business doing what they're trying to do. They see me as an easy target. Someone they can do what they want with and not have a care in the world. I will surprise them all. I need to make not only my mind stronger but my body as well.

There's one thing I can do while I sit and wait. I head into the clubhouse to find Torch. He's the only one I can think of here to help me with what I want to do. Being the enforcer of the club, he knows how to defend himself and fight. I want control back and my mind is made up. I find Torch sitting at the bar nursing a drink.

"Torch," I call to him. He turns his head and pierces me with bright blue eyes. The scowl on his bearded face disappears when he spots me.

"What can I do for you, Danyella?" The deep rasp of his voice is soothing. His scarred hands clenching his glass is a contradiction to the calm facade he's putting forth.

Taking a deep breath I exhale, gaining the confidence I need to ask what I want to ask. "Can you teach me how to fight and defend myself?"

"No." Torch turns his back to me; his leather cut creaks under protest.

All the confidence I had deflates and my shoulders sag. "I get it. A woman in the ring isn't good for the club." Anger fills my voice causing his hands to clench harder around the glass. "That's OK. I'll find Bear or Red and ask them. But I figured you'd be able to help me. Must be you're all talk and no action." I turn my back on him and start to walk away.

"Wait a fucking minute, little one." Torch stands to his full height, dwarfing me. He releases a deep sigh, "Fuck me, I'm asking for trouble. Meet me at the gym in ten. You want to learn to fight, I'll teach you. But don't cry when it gets tough." Torch walks past me toward his room and I hurry into mine.

I change into workout shorts and a sports bra. I'm tying my shoes when Monica comes sauntering in my room and plops on the bed next to me.

"What are you doing?"

"Torch is teaching me to fight." The excitement in my voice is unmistakable.

Capone's Chaos

Her eyebrows raise high into her forehead. "Are you sure that's a good idea?"

"Why wouldn't it be? I need to learn how to defend myself." I sigh before standing up.

"Because it's not my brother teaching you." Monica answers. I turn to look at her, trying to figure out what she's talking about. "Look, I know you don't get it, but having another man teach you to fight isn't a good idea."

"Why not? It's not like Derek has any interest in me. He's made that clear." I cross my arms over my chest, irritated. "Besides, I'm not looking to hook up with Torch. I need to get control of my life back. If I knew how to defend myself, I never would've been taken."

"Oh, Danyella you have no clue, do you?" The pity in Monica's eyes has the hair on my arm stand on end.

"Clue about what? What are you talking about?"

"Nothing. Just watch what you're doing. You're asking a brother to train you and that brother isn't the one you want." Monica rises from the bed and we walk together into the common's room.

"I'm so confused, Monica. What aren't you telling me?" I stop and rest a hand on her arm. "Please, tell me."

J. Lynn Lombard

She offers me a sweet smile and pats my hand. "It's not my place to say anything. Derek will tell you when he's ready."

"Danyella, you ready?" Torch asks, interrupting our conversation. He has on a pair of basketball shorts, no shirt, displaying all his tattoos and muscles, and a pair of shoes. He looks different without his jeans and leather cut.

"Are you sure this is a good idea?" Monica asks.

"Yup, little one wants to learn how to defend herself. Why shouldn't I teach her?" A look passes between the two of them. If I wasn't paying attention, I would've missed it.

"Fine, I'll join you. Blayze has taught me a lot in the last few years that could be helpful." Monica speaks up.

"You don't have to, Monica, I'll be fine." I'm not sure what's going on but for some reason, she doesn't want me alone with Torch. It's not like I have any interest in him. He's not the one who makes my heart skip in my chest or my brain to stop working.

"I have nothing else to do while I wait for Blayze to get back. Besides, it'll be fun." Monica leaves to change.

"Ready?" Torch asks again. With a nod of my head, I follow Torch out the back door and into the gym. He flips on a light and leads me to the treadmills set up along the wall. "First you're going to warm up those leg muscles. Run for fifteen, get the heart pumping, then we'll move to the arms."

"I thought we were going to fight?" I'm confused.

"We will, little one, but you can't just jump right in. You want my help; this is how we'll do it." Torch sets the treadmill while I get on. "When you get moving, increase the speed every five minutes until you're maxed out."

The treadmill moves under my feet and I begin walking. Increasing the speed every few minutes until I'm jogging, sweat pouring off me like never before. Torch moves to the back of the gym, out of sight. I hear his phone ring but can't hear what he says.

Monica enters the gym and jumps on the treadmill next to me. She adjusts her speed and starts jogging right away. I increase the speed on mine some more until I'm running, Monica does the same. We keep pace with each other until Torch comes back and slows me down, Monica follows and once we slow down enough to walk, we shut the treadmills off.

"This way," Torch grumbles and I follow him to a set of weights. My legs are on fire but I won't complain. He hands me a set of small hand weights and I begin curling. "Two reps of ten, then two more reps of ten on each hand. Monica, you have a sec?"

J. Lynn Lombard

Torch motions with his head and they walk into the back of the gym. I can't hear what they're saying no matter how hard I try. Monica comes back out with Torch on her heels. She smiles at me and begins her reps. Once we're done, I follow them into the back of the gym.

He has the boxing area set up with a jump rope, a big rope, punching bags and body bags. That's what those big bags look like to me. He's going to torture me until I can't move, isn't he?

Torch stands next to the jump rope and picks it up, threading it through his fingers, "In order to be a good fighter and defend yourself, you need agility." He hands me the jump rope. "The faster your feet move, the better you can counteract your opponent's strikes. I want five sets of ten."

I take the jump rope out of his hands. This isn't what I was thinking I had to do to defend myself. I begin my sets, first slowly then picking up speed as I go. Torch watches from the corner of the room.

"Good, keep it up. Before long, these will be easy." Torch appraises.

"I didn't realize I'm this out of shape," I pant. Sweat is pouring off me in buckets.

"You're not that out of shape, you don't use these muscles. Which is what I'm fixing. We'll do this at the same time every day. And if I'm not here for some reason, you'll do it alone or with Monica. No excuses. I'll know if you cheat yourself." Torch says.

He walks to the back of the room and turns on the radio. Music pumping out of the speakers gets me motivated to move faster. My reps are done and I'm panting and out of breath.

"What's next?" I ask holding my hands above my head. My legs are on fire and my lungs burn.

"Next is the rope." Torch demonstrates what I need to do with this big thing. I don't know if I can even wrap my hands around the thing it's so big. He holds one in each hand and moves one arm then the other, creating a ripple with the rope. "You try. Give me what you can with this one and we'll adjust as we go."

I step up and grab it. My fingers barely wrap around the thickness of it and begin swinging my arms trying to mimic Torch. After ten minutes, my back is aching and I can barely lift my arms. This ass is trying to kill me, I know it for sure now.

"OK, good. Now, I'm going to tape up your hands and you're going to show me how you punch." Torch motions for me to come over and I do, dragging my feet. He tapes my hands up with some white sticky tape on one side. I've seen MMA fighters use this before but never knew why. "This will protect your knuckles and help keep your wrists strong." Torch finishes taping up my hands and he does the same to Monica. I take a quick water break while I wait, guzzling the bottle as fast as I can. Torch shakes his head like he knows something I don't. I crush the water bottle and stand in the center of the room.

"First, I want you to show me your stance."

I want to show him I know what I'm doing, so I recall what someone taught me years ago. I think it was some guy I tried to date in high school. That didn't last long for some unknown reason. I stand with my feet shoulder-width apart and bring my fists up next to my face. My right arm is out a little further than my left. Torch walks around me and grabs my hips, pivoting them. He immediately drops them like I burned him. He kicks my legs out a little further with his toes. He grabs my hands and adjusts my fists so they're a little lower than before. Minimal contact and he's squirming in his shorts. What the hell?

"Are you left or right-handed?" Torch's rough voice asks.

"Left."

"This will be a little odd for me, but I'll make it work. Keep your hands just below your chin. Your right hand stays slightly higher than your left and away from your body. Your left hand will be level with your collar bone and closer to your body." Torch instructs.

I make the adjustments. "It feels weird."

Capone's Chaos

"That's because your muscle memory is set to the other way. We'll work on it so it comes naturally." Torch stands in front of me. "Now, punch with your left. Bring it across your body and move your right in slightly." I do what he says and he grabs my fist, turning it. "When you punch, you want it straight, not curved or turned. You'll break your hand or wrist if you don't." I do it again.

"Good, keep that up." I repeat the process several times until he tells me to stop. "Now, do the same with your right." I do and find myself adjusting my wrist as I extend it. "Feet apart!" Torch shouts. I move my feet where he had them. "Now do both, left and then right."

Hours later I have the new technique down, my arms are sore and I can barely keep them raised. My feet are aching and my lungs are burning. Monica has been doing the exact same thing right next to me. Only she isn't sweating as bad as I am.

"Take a break and we'll come back at it again tomorrow." Torch instructs. I drop my arms and fall onto the mat covering my eyes with my tired arms.

"How in the hell do you do this torture?" I groan.

"I've been doing it for years," Monica plops down next to me and hands me a water. "Here drink this. You'll need to drink lots of water so your muscles don't seize and cramp on you."

"I can't move," I attempt to grab the bottle but fail miserably. "Too tired."

Monica laughs before helping me sit up. "Here, now you can." I take the offered water and guzzle it down. "Slow down, Champ. You'll make yourself sick."

My stomach turns as soon as she says that. Bile climbing its way up my throat, burning it. Monica puts a bucket under my chin and I immediately throw up the water I just drank. "Uh…" I groan, setting the bucket next to me.

"Small sips, girl. Small sips."

"Where's Torch?" I ask looking around the gym. There are no windows at this level so it's hard to say what time it is.

"He left right after you laid down." Monica shrugs her shoulders.

"He really hates doing this doesn't he?" Sadness laces my voice.

"No, it's not that. It's hard to explain," Monica answers.

"What's hard to explain? Either he wants to help me or he doesn't. It's not that hard."

Monica runs her hands down her face and sighs. "You need to talk to Derek, that's all I can say." She stands up and stretches her arms above her head. The scars on her stomach are peeking out when her shirt raises. With everything this girl has been through, the scars she carries, she still managed to find love and take back control.

"How'd you do it?" I blurt out the question.

"Do what?"

"Overcome everything that's happened to you?"

"The same way you will. I had the support of my brother and Blayze, the club, and most importantly, I learned how to love myself. No matter what happened to me, it didn't define me but it gave me strength to fight through all the self-doubt."

"Do you really think I can do it?" I ask hopefully.

"I know you will. When your mind is ready you can and will take everything that's happened to you and become a stronger woman." Monica gently squeezes my arm and helps me up. Together we walk out of the gym and into the fading sun.

"Wow, we've been in there for quite some time." My stomach growls in protest. "I'm a little hungry." Monica and I both giggle.

She leans into me and sniffs. "You need a shower. You smell really bad."

"So do you." I counter with a laugh.

J. Lynn Lombard

She sniffs herself, "Oh my God, you're right. Shower, dinner then we can relax with a movie. I don't know about you but with Blayze gone, I really don't want to be alone tonight."

"I don't want to be alone either," I confess. I have nightmares every night and sleep usually evades me. No one knows about my struggles and I don't plan on telling anyone either. There's only one way that I've been able to sleep since I've been back. One night a while back, I couldn't sleep and my mind was overtaken with so much bad shit, I found myself in front of Derek's door. He could have told me to leave, but he didn't. Instead, he let me in and comforted me. Nothing happened that night, but I did manage to sleep all night long. Little things like that and the way he watches me when I'm near sets my skin on fire. Then he turns cold and it's no wonder I'm confused about where we stand.

"Good, I'll meet you in the kitchen in twenty. I'll go tell one of the patch whores to make us something." Monica takes off into the clubhouse before I can say anything.

I stay on the back porch and soak up the fading sun, relaxing and finding a little bit of peace. A breeze washes over my skin, bringing the salty sea air with it. I release a deep sigh and head inside to my room.

I know I need to talk to someone about what happened, but I don't know who I can trust. Who won't judge me and look at me with pity. There is

Capone's Chaos

one person who I want to trust and talk to. With my mind made up, I grab my phone off my dresser. I have one voice mail and six text messages. I ignore the voicemail, not wanting to go down that road and begin scrolling through the messages with a smile on my face. All six are from Derek. I send a quick response, grab some clothes and head into the shower with an extra skip in my step. Maybe there is a chance for us.

J. Lynn Lombard

Chapter 5

Capone

We touch down in NOLA airport and Jameson has a prospect waiting to take us back to his clubhouse deep in the swamp. The pickup we're in is built for backroad bogging, which is what we're currently doing.

"How in the fuck do you bring a bike down these roads?" I grumble. The prospect, who's name I didn't bother with, hits another bump and my teeth rattle in my head.

"We don't. There's another road built just for bikes. No cages allowed." The prospect answers.

"Fuck this dumbass backwoods shit," Blayze mumbles from the backseat. The prospect hits anther fucking bump and Blayze hits his head on the roof of the pickup. "I swear to the motherfucking biker Gods, if I hit this roof one more time, I'm going to knock your teeth so far down your throat, you'll be shoving a toothbrush up your ass to brush your teeth, prospect."

Capone's Chaos

The prospect eases up on the gas and the rest of the ride is smoother. Once we reach the end of the road, a clearing comes into view with the National Chapter's Clubhouse directly in front of me. A line of bikes is parked in front along with a few other beefed up trucks. We're surrounded by trees and I can hear the critters in the bayou off in the distance. Jameson steps out of the clubhouse, slamming the door behind him.

I climb out of the pickup and approach him, "Good to see you, brother." We bro hug and slap each other on the back. Blayze and Jameson do the same thing.

"Glad the two of you could make it. We have a surprise for all of you," Jameson gestures for us to enter his Clubhouse.

Once we make it inside, my jaw drops and a huge smile lights up my face. Every single President and V.P. are here, drinking, talking and shooting the shit. Demon and Drake from the Savannah Chapter, Mason and Carson from the Birmingham, AL Chapter, Murder from Charleston, WV, Petros and Helix from the Lincoln, NE chapter. Petros has had some issues with a woman but apparently, the new one he found is doing good for him. He looks better than what he did last time I saw him. Declan and Axel from the Flagstaff, AZ Chapter, Ghoul and Crow from the Cleveland Chapter are here. I see Crow texting on his phone with a shit eating grin in his face. Nycto and Void from our Tampa Chapter are here. The fuckers

J. Lynn Lombard

Koyn and Filter are here from Tulsa, OK, two of my favorite assholes. Crucifix and Rattler from the NYC Chapter are here. Crucifix gives me a nod of the head. We had some business a few months back and thanks to Blayze, their girl Nixx is bringing in a lot of money-making RB porn. Grim and Mammoth from Tonopah give me a nod and a slap on the back. They also helped us out when we had a lead on Bloody Scorpions in their area. We were a day late but got to catch up with them. Hornet and Silver from the Detroit Chapter are standing toward the back of the room. Dog and Burn from Idaho Springs and Edge from Santa Fe are here also.

The only one I notice missing is Gamble. She's the only woman to hold a Prez spot in the Royal Bastards. I know Rancid did it intentionally to try and shame and humiliate her and our club. The only thing he didn't count on was most of us backing her up and helping her when she needed it. Most of us will do anything for that woman. She's been through hell and back no thanks to Rancid and his fucked-up pedophile dick. Which is why we're all here gathered under one roof for the first time ever.

Jameson enters the room and whistles loudly. "You fuckers know why all your ugly mugs are here today. We're going to put an end to the one person who fooled so many of us throughout the years." He nods to Knuckles and Knuckles leaves the room only to come back a few minutes later, dragging a kicking and screaming Rancid by his hair. My blood pressure rises at the sight of the motherfucker. "You'll get your chance." Jameson gives me a wink and a nod of his head.

After what this asshole has done to me and my club, I'm going to enjoy every swing of the bat. Every drop of blood and I'll finally get peace watching the life drain from his eyes. Rancid tried strong arming his way into my club and tried to take a few of my girls for his own sick pleasure right after I took over as Prez. Apparently, Chains had an agreement with him for years. Rancid would come in, take his pick, the younger the better and leave with her only to never be seen again. After I took over, that fucking shit stopped, pissing Rancid off in the process. I banned him from ever stepping foot in my territory again. I've been waiting for the day it's my turn to get revenge on all the girls he took against their will.

"Capone, you're up," Jameson hands me the bat and I take it in my hands. Already coated with blood from the other presidents getting their revenge, I hold the bat back and swing with everything I have. The satisfying crunch of bone against wood settles the beast resting inside my chest. I watch Rancid's blood drip from his busted mouth and not a drop of remorse comes to me. This fucker deserves everything he's getting. I hand the bat off to Jameson and stand to the back.

The front door opens and the final piece of the puzzle comes into play. Gamble walks in with her swollen belly and heads right for Rancid. Taking pleasure of everything she does to him I watch as she exacts revenge on him for taking away Dog, the love of her life. She takes back the power Rancid held over her and now I understand why Danyella and Monica did what they did in Michigan. I understand everything as I watch Rancid take his last breath.

***

Once everyone clears out and heads off to do their own thing, Blayze and I go to the hotel we're staying at. He's in the bathroom taking a shower and I'm pacing back and forth on the worn carpet, trying to figure out how to fix the situation with Danyella. Does she want some kind of grand gesture or would she rather I do subtle? Does she even want to pursue something with me or am I wasting my time?

Throwing caution to the wind, I send her a text.

Me: There are some things we need to talk about when I get back.

I press send and wait. Then I wait some more. When she doesn't answer right away, I send another one.

Me: Look I know you're still mad at me about last night. I would rather talk to you face to face about it.

When she doesn't answer me back, paranoia sets in. What the hell is she doing? Is she staring at her phone waiting for me to text her like I am right now or is she laughing at my attempt of an apology?

Capone's Chaos

What the fuck am I doing? I don't chase anyone, I'm the motherfucking Prez for Christ sakes. No woman should have this much power over me.

My phone rings in my hand and it's Torch on the other end. I swipe the green button to answer, "Torch."

"Prez. Got a dilemma here." I can hear echoing of feet in the background.

"What's up?"

"Uh… not sure how to put it." Torch exhales sending my blood pressure up, "Danyella asked me to teach her how to fight." He blurts out. That's the last thing I thought he'd say.

I'm speechless. Images of Belle in a pair of tight shorts and a sports bra with sweat dripping down her luscious body has my cock hard. Her grunts and moans vibrating the air sends a wave of lust rolling through my body.

"Prez, you there?" Torch sounds unsure of himself.

I adjust my cock and clear my throat. "Yeah, I'm here. That's all she wants is to learn how to defend herself?"

"Yes."

"Then do it. But, by all that is holy and sacred to you, I will cut off your dick if you touch her." I growl.

J. Lynn Lombard

"How do I train her with no contact?"

"I don't give a fuck, figure it out. But if you lay a hand on her, I will cut it off and beat you with it." I end the call and shove my phone in my cut. Now I know why she isn't answering me and feel like an idiot for the self-doubt I've caused.

Blayze comes out of the bathroom with a towel around his waist and steam following close behind. "Shower's yours if you want it." He grabs his bag and drops his towel, changing into clean clothes.

Looking down at my scarred knuckles from years of fighting, I think about Danyella and how I've screwed up so many times with her. I rub my right thumb over my left knuckles lost in thought. I'm still trying to figure out how to fix us, I grab my phone and send her another text. Not sure it'll do what I want it to, I send 3 more, hoping it'll bring a smile to her face and make her miss me as much as I miss her.

I toss my phone onto the table and head into the bathroom. I need a shower and some food before we head to bed and take off in the morning. All this flying coast to coast is going to catch up with me if I don't take care of myself. Finished with my shower, I leave the bathroom and get dressed. Blayze is talking on his phone with Monica and I roll my eyes with the vulgar shit he's saying to her. I swear if they weren't married and he wasn't my best friend, I'd knock his teeth down his throat. Blayze hangs up his phone after several I love you's and I miss you's.

Capone's Chaos

"Where do you want to eat?" He asks.

"I don't give a fuck." I answer. Yes, I'm jealous. I want what he has but Danyella still hasn't answered my text yet.

"Seen a bar down the street. Let's go there."

I look down at my phone hoping she answered and disappointment fills me. "Yeah, whatever." I put my phone in the inside of my cut and we leave the hotel room.

The sweltering heat of Louisiana makes my clothes stick to me. We find the bar and settle into a booth in the corner. The waitress takes our orders and leaves after trying to flirt with us but failing. I might be single but I'm not on the market and she just doesn't do it for me.

"What's going on Prez? You've been moody and quiet lately. Worse than normal." Blayze asks. He has no clue how I feel about his sister and I don't think he ever had. The waitress brings us our beer and appetizers and I take a long pull. "Is it Danyella?" Blayze asks.

I choke on my beer and spit some of it back out in shock. "What?" I ask once I can talk again.

Blayze grabs a mozzarella stick and chews before answering. His green eyes like his sisters assess me. "I've seen the way you watch her. How you know where she is at all times and don't think I didn't see you sneaking off at my wedding last night. You two were practically fucking on the dance floor."

Speechless, I take another drink and figure out a way to answer him. Blayze speaks before I do. "Look, I get it. She's been through a lot of shit and you don't want to drag her down with you." He wipes his hands on a napkin, takes a pull of his beer before continuing. "But denying her what you each want isn't good for either of you. She needs to heal and you need her light. Don't wait too long before she decides you don't want her anymore." Blayze stands, "I need to piss."

He walks toward the bathroom and I know he's right. I'm trying here. I know I'll fuck up and make mistakes. But I won't give up. Not yet. My phone buzzes in my cut and my heart skips a beat, fucking thing. I yank my phone out and see my Belle flash across the screen. I open the text she sent and a real smile lights up my face. It's a picture of her in her tiny shorts and sports bra, sweat glistening off her body. Her text has my blood pumping and my cock instantly hard. Under the picture she wrote:

My Belle: Don't wait too long, Derek. I see you and I'm ready.

I instantly write her back, my fingers flying over the keypad.

Me: I'll be home tomorrow. I want to see that little outfit in my room. We need to have a serious convo about where we're heading.

Capone's Chaos

> My Belle: Is that all?
>
> Me: For now. Think of me when you sleep tonight. When you're touching yourself, think of my hands, lips and mouth all over that tight little body. Think about how I'll ravish you with my tongue and make you scream my name as you come all over my face.
>
> My Belle: Hmm... I'm thinking of you right now while I'm taking a shower. Will that work?
>
> Me: Woman, I'm sitting in a bar trying to eat. You're killing me here.
>
> My Belle: I have something else you can eat.
>
> Me: Oh, I'll be eating all right. As soon as my feet hit the Clubhouse floor you better be ready. I'm done waiting and trying to be good to you.
>
> My Belle: I don't want you to be good, Derek. I want you. I want you as you are. The good, the bad and the dirty.
>
> Me: Then you'll have me. Blayze is back. I've got to go and try to calm this raging hard-on I have before he sees it.
>
> My Belle: That'll be a little awkward. Having a boner while eating dinner with my brother.
>
> Me: And putting that image in my head, it's gone down.

J. Lynn Lombard

> **My Belle: Glad I could help. I'll see you tomorrow.**

> **Me: Good night beautiful. I see you tomorrow.**

Blayze takes his seat and digs into his food, ignoring the smile on my face. He chews and swallows before speaking. "What did Scorch want earlier?"

"We have to head South when we get back. I have a job for Torch while we're there." I answer.

"Does this have anything to do with what you found on Chains in the rundown warehouse?"

Back when we found out where the Bloody Scorpions were holding Danyella and all the other girls for trafficking, Chains, the old Prez of our Chapter, ended up being the one behind all of it. He was at the warehouse the night we rescued them and I ended his life. He had a photograph on him that turned my blood to ice. I knew as soon as I saw it, my mother was in danger. I made a few phone calls and have people I trust watching her home. So far, it's been quiet but I won't put anything past Chains and the Salazar Cartel to have another plan in place, even in death.

"Everything to do with that. I'll hold Church tomorrow and get everyone filled in. I know you and Monica just got married, but I need you with me, brother."

Capone's Chaos

"I won't miss it for the world. Those fuckers are going down for threatening the club and your mother like that." The edge in Blayze's voice settles the anxiety I have about protecting her. She really screwed everything up the night she told me Chains wasn't my father, but I'm thankful I don't have his blood running through my veins.

We finish our dinner, pay for it and head back to the hotel. Tomorrow will be a long day of traveling and planning our next move. The longer we wait, the more danger my Club and family are in. Time is not on our side anymore.

J. Lynn Lombard

Chapter 6

Capone

Our plane touched down at LAX later the next night and the ride back to the clubhouse was uneventful. That was until we hit the clubhouse doors. Now music is pumping through the speakers, everyone is partying and celebrating mine and Blayze's return. Alcohol, weed and cigarette smoke is thick in the air. Patch whores are dancing on every available surface, hoping to gain the attention of a brother.

I release an internal groan and I know Blayze feels the same. The last thing either of us wants to do is party. He wants to be buried balls deep in his Ol' Lady before we head to Mexico and I want to find Danyella. After our heated texting last night, the urge to find her is strong. I don't know how she'll react to me face to face.

A pair of warm hand run up and down my exposed arms, racking her nails along my skin. "You look like you can use a little reprieve, Capone." The sultry voice of a patch whore, Rose, whispers in my ear. "Come with me and I'll take the edge off."

I don't respond and take a seat at the bar with Rose following behind me. She wedges herself between me and the bar top and tries sitting on my lap. I don't make it easy on her but she's like a bull who sees red. She won't give up.

"I'm not interested." Red's prospect, Bones is manning the bar again and slides a glass of whiskey in my direction.

"You can't mean that Prez. Use me to make yourself forget." Rose's tits press against my arm and she nibbles on my ear. Bile climbs its way up my throat. "I can make you feel wanted, unlike Danyella."

A few nights ago, Danyella walked away from me, angry and heartbroken and hasn't looked in my direction since. We've exchanged heated text messages last night and the last thing she has done is make me feel unwanted. If anything, she's driving me insane to find her. I finish my drink and spot her in the middle of the dance floor. She's looking at me with lust and longing in her emerald eyes which are currently staring at me, taking my breath away. She hasn't blessed me with her sweet smile or her light laughter in days and I'm like a drug addict, I need it all the time. I don't blame her either. I was a dickhead and deserve it all taken away from me. But damn it, it hurt. I deserve this pain in my chest. All

J. Lynn Lombard

the bad shit I've done. All the blood spilled by my hands. All of it. I don't deserve anything from someone created as an angel. But fuck me, I'm taking it anyways.

I shove Rose off me and she falls on her ass with a thud and a cry. I don't even bother to check if she's all right. My boots eat up the distance of the room until I'm in Danyella's space. Her breath catches in her throat but she doesn't break eye contact. I'm done being the nice guy and holding back.

"Belle," I whisper. My breath carrying across her face. "If you're ready for me, be prepared. I won't stop until I have your full submission."

A flush spreads across her porcelain skin. The music fades away, voices disappear as I stare into Danyella's eyes, willing her to give me the green light. Begging her to give in to this attraction we have towards each other.

One word. That's all I need. One word from her plump red lips to put us both out of this misery. Only, that word never comes. Shots ring out through my clubhouse destroying everything in their path. I yank Danyella down and cover her body with my own, shielding her from the bullets ripping through the clubhouse. Screams and cries echo around me as I protect my woman.

I pop my head up and pull my .40 caliber out of the inside of my cut. I can't see who's doing the shooting, but from the sounds, several automatics are spraying around us.

"Stay here and keep covered," I command Danyella. She nods her head, tears streaming down her face.

"Derek, wait." Danyella grabs my cut and pulls me in for a heated kiss. One I want to keep going, but I can't. "Stay safe."

I nod my head, speechless, and crawl my way to Blayze, Torch, Bear and Tiny. They flipped a pool table over and are using it for shelter from the onslaught. Monica and Daisy are nowhere in sight. I raise an eyebrow to Blayze and he points toward the bar. Monica is helping Danyella and the three of them are crawling behind it for safety. I exhale a sigh of relief.

"Let's end these motherfuckers." I growl. Adrenaline is pouring through my blood, itching to attack. Shots still ring out, destroying my commons room. "Cover me."

Blayze peeks around the left side of the pool table, Tiny does the same on the right. They both begin firing in the area the shots are coming from. The brutal onslaught to my clubhouse slows down as one of their bullets hits its mark. I stand and run from my spot to the couch and slide across the concrete floor. My feet slip in blood but I don't have time to figure out who's it is right now. Shots ring out over my head and another bullet hits the intended target.

J. Lynn Lombard

I fire into the hallway leading to our bikes and the return bullets suddenly stop.

My ears are ringing and the smell of acid and copper heavy in the air. Moans and whimpers are heavy in the air but I don't see who's hit. Not yet. I stalk my way toward the area the unknown men were and Blayze, Torch and Bear are hot on my heels. One man is slouched against the wall, streaks of blood behind him. He's not moving. I check for a pulse anyway with a shaky hand and confirm he's dead. Behind him is another man. His brains are scattered along the wall behind him. No need to check for a pulse. A grunt and a thud further down the hallway draw my attention and I follow the blood trail. Whoever this belongs too isn't dead yet, but that will change once I get my hands on him. Fading sunlight filters into the garage from the rolling doors and there's no sign of the injured shooter anywhere.

Squealing of tires on asphalt draws my attention and I hurry over to the open doors just as taillights disappear. I fire my gun at the van, running in their direction, but they're too far away to hit. The gates leading into my clubhouse are off the track and a prospect's body is slumped forward. I check his pulse, he's dead.

"What now, Prez?" Tiny asks.

"Now we figure out who these dick suckers are." I stomp back into the garage leading into the clubhouse. Fury replaces the adrenaline and the need to hurt someone is radiating off me in waves. "Fix

Capone's Chaos

those fucking gates and put two people on them asap. This will not happen again!" I slam my fist into the concrete wall. The pain penetrating through the fury, helping me think straight.

Tiny and Dagger disappear with their prospects hot on their heels. Each member, besides myself and Blayze, has a prospect they're vouching for to gain a spot into our club. If these two can hold their own and prove their worth in the club, they'll be patched in. It might be sooner rather than later with the destruction that just happened.

I kick a broken beer bottle out of my way and turn to Red who's at the bar slamming back a shot. "Find out who those fuckers are and what club they're affiliated with. Find out where their momma's sleep and how they like to fuck. Leave nothing unturned."

"On it, Prez." Red slams his glass down on the bar and disappears out of sight. He comes back a few minutes later with two fingers and a smirk, heading into the communications room he has set up.

"Capone?" A quiet voice echoes around the room and I spot Danyella, Monica and Daisy huddled together in the hallway. They're holding each other tight with tears streaming down their faces. I hurry over to them and scoop Danyella up into my arms. Fuck what anyone thinks. I almost lost her tonight and I'll be damned if I let her go again. Blayze grabs Monica and Daisy looks uncomfortable.

J. Lynn Lombard

"Are you hurt?" I ask brushing Danyella's long blonde hair out of her face. Her emerald eyes are red from her tears. She shakes her head no and releases a deep breath, resting her head on my chest. I stroke her hair, keeping her close.

"Prez, we need to get this cleaned up." Torch approaches us from behind and I take in the devastation surrounding me. Bullets destroyed the couches, TV, pool tables and walls. It's going to take a lot of labor, but we can do it. A few patch whores are standing around, kicking broken things out of their way. Some are bleeding, others are stunned at what just happened.

"I'll help," Daisy speaks up and disappears into the kitchen. She comes back out with garbage bags, gloves, buckets and cleaning products. Trigger hurries over and helps her with everything.

"We'll help too," Monica gives Blayze a heated kiss and whispers something to him. He grunts and slaps her on her retreating ass.

Danyella is still pressed against me, the feel of her soft curves has my cock wanting attention and I peer down at her. She looks up at me with hunger in her eyes. I brush her hair out of her face again and she licks her lips. My eyes follow the trail of her wet tongue and a groan escapes the back of my throat. This isn't the time for my dick to do the talking but this woman is driving me crazy.

Capone's Chaos

"Are you OK?" Danyella quietly asks, her eyes watching mine.

I cup her face with both hands and her breathing picks up. "I'm fine. A little pissed off that this happened. This isn't how I imagined our night to go."

Danyella giggles and it's music to my ears. "If Rose didn't back off, it would've been worse."

"That I don't doubt, Belle." Fuck waiting. I waited for her to give me the word last time and look what happened. I lean in and press my lips against hers. All the doubts running through my head disappear with Danyella's lips compliant against mine. Finally, my head and my cock are on the same page. Danyella sighs when I kiss her, opening her mouth for me to explore. I thread my fingers through her hair, swallowing up her moans. Her taste is on my tongue and I want more. I need more.

Danyella digs her nails into my dark hair and a groan rumbles from deep within. It's primal with need and hunger. Kissing my Belle is like heaven. Her soft lips against mine, her tongue moving with mine, battling back and forth. The whimpers and moans she produces drive me crazy.

A throat clears behind me, loud and annoyed. I break the kiss with Danyella, panting and rest my forehead against hers. "We'll continue this later, Belle. Club calls." She nods her head. I've made her speechless and my chest swells with pride. Releasing the grip I have on her head, I turn to see Blayze staring at me with fire in his eyes. He should've known I wasn't holding back any longer. Danyella is mine and I will do everything in my power to protect her.

"You got a second, Prez?" The way he grits out my title brings a smirk to my lips pissing him off more. Take that asshole. Now you know how I felt each time I watched you lust after my sister.

"Yeah," I turn to Danyella. The lust and longing in her eyes is my undoing. "Wait for me, please?" This time I ask instead of demand. I've discovered when you ask her to do something, she'll be more compliant.

"I'll help the girls clean up. Come find me when you're done." She saunters off to help Monica, Daisy and the patch whores. I watch her ass sway the whole time until she's out of sight.

"What'd you need?" I play coy with Blayze to see where this is going.

"I need to know what the fuck you're doing. Are you sure you want to play this game?" The gruffness in Blayze's voice draws my attention to him. He's staring at me with trepidation in his eyes.

"I get you're worried about your sister. But I have no intention of hurting her." I rest my hands on my hips and exhale a deep breath. "Do you remember when she was missing?"

Capone's Chaos

"Yeah," Blayze looks at me with confusion all over his face.

"Well, do you remember how pissed the fuck off I was and how no one could calm me down?" Blayze nods his head and I continue. "That's because she wasn't here. I found my other half the moment the two of you walked into these doors. She didn't want to accept it then, but she's ready to accept it now. Danyella is mine. Always has been. Always will be."

"What about the whores you've fucked when she was missing?"

"I didn't fuck any of them. I couldn't." I confess.

Blayze holds up a hand, "Wait. Let me get this straight. The one time I went to your office, it smelled like sex and a half-naked patch whore ran out. You're telling me you didn't fuck her?"

"Nope," I answer popping the p. "She fucked herself on my couch, trying to get me to do it. She was mortified when she realized it wasn't working." I stare at Blayze, "Listen, I'm not telling you this for pity or anything else. You all think I'm a man-whore and I let you think that way. If our enemies know what Danyella means to me, she'll be in danger. Which is why I've kept her at arm's length. But I'm done pretending. And after what happened tonight? There's no way in hell I'm letting these moments I can have with her disappear. They almost did twice. I'm done pretending."

"It's about fucking time." Blayze slaps a hand on my shoulder, squeezing it tight. "It's about fucking time." He releases my shoulder, "Tiny and Dagger are almost done fixing the gates. When do you want to call Church?"

"Let's see what Red's up to and go from there. I want answers before the rest of the Club asks questions. We also need to discuss Mexico."

"Have you told Monica about your mom?"

"Not yet. I don't want to put any more stress on her until I can give her clear answers."

"Don't wait too long, Derek. You know how she gets when something like this is hidden from her."

"I know. Trust me, I know. C'mon, let's go see what Red's figured out and then get all the brothers together for Church."

Blayze and I walk into Red's communication room. His big body is hunched over and he has all his computers on and his fingers are flying over the keyboards. The screens all have a bunch of numbers on them scrolling faster than his fingers are typing.

Another screen off to the right is flipping through images. I'm guessing it's to find whoever in the fuck these guys were. A screen to the left has the

Capone's Chaos

images of all the girls we rescued. Most of them have returned home, others stayed here hoping to find a home. The ones that were held captive the longest are the ones who've had a hard time integrating into the real world and we've done what we can to help them. The little girl, Aerial, who was with Danyella and Daisy is still here. We still haven't located her mother yet. But there's something about her that seems so familiar and I can't figure out why.

"What do you have, Red?" I ask.

Red pulls his head up and his fingers pause over the keys. His eyes are flickering back and forth between each monitor. "I'm running a check on the fingerprints from those two dick fuckers out there. I'm also running facial recognition on the one who got away. Our security cameras picked them up entering the clubhouse. Here, let me show you."

Red presses a button on a keyboard and the screen directly in front of us lights up and plays like a silent movie. The nondescript van backs up to the gate and the rear doors open. The prospect is perched on the roof holding his AR15 shouting at the people in the van. They open fire on the prospect and he slumps forward before diving head first off the roof. Dead before he hit the ground.

Rage is consuming my every pore as I continue watching. The back of the van smashes into the gates a few times before they knock it off the rollers and they back in. Turning around, they drive fast toward the entrance to our clubhouse. Three men climb out of the van with their faces covered and AK47's at their hips. The first guy picks the lock on the door and then the garage door opens. The van backs up to the doors and the three men come inside. We know what happens after that and Red stops the tape.

"Anything on who they are?" I ask through clenched teeth.

"Waiting for the programs to pick something up." As soon as Red says that, one of his computers beeps at him. "Bingo! Got you, you sorry piece of shit assholes." Red mutters to himself. The printer spits out several pieces of paper and Red grabs them off the tray.

He hands them to me and I read the print outs. My stomach sinks into my toes. "Jesus Matteo and Anton Garcia. Low ranking members of the Salazar Cartel. Both have been popped for kidnapping, breaking and entering and drug possession over the last few years." Shit, this isn't good. I have secrets that not even Blayze knows about and if these two fuckers are here, it means Salazar has figured out about Danyella.

"Does this mean what I think it means?" Blayze asks.

"Yeah. We're definitely heading to Mexico. Handle business for Scorch, then our own. These

Capone's Chaos

motherfuckers just messed with the wrong Royal Bastard."

J. Lynn Lombard

Chapter 7

Danyella

Helping the girls clean up the clubhouse, the taste of Capone is still on my tongue sending butterflies to roll through my stomach and my panties are damp. One kiss from him and I'm a pile of goo lost in my own little world. What I wouldn't give to have his tongue and lips all over my body taking me places I've never gone before. I'm not innocent by any means, but no man has made my body sing the way Derek does. He makes me crave him in ways I've never lusted after a man before. He's been patient, waiting for me to get my head on straight and he deserves all I can give him.

Rose approaches me with hesitant steps and I stop sweeping up the debris watching her. "Danyella, can I have a word?"

I set the broom aside and give her my attention. "Sure."

"I want to apologize for earlier. If I had known the two of you were a thing, I never would've hit on Capone." Her eyes cast to the floor as her foot plays with a piece of the wall, rolling it back and forth. "Can I be honest with you?"

"I'd rather you were honest than a snake."

"I've tried in the past to, you know, do things with him, but he's never given me the time of day. I figured it was me and there was something wrong with me, but after watching what he did to protect you tonight, Capone has never done that with anyone before besides his sister."

"What are you getting at Rose? You're rambling." I'm confused as hell at what she's trying to say. "Just spit it out already."

Rose releases a deep breath and squares her shoulders, her eyes finally meeting mine. "What I'm trying to ask is, can you forgive me for hitting on Capone all this time and not realizing where his head really is. The last thing I want or need is to have his Ol' Lady kicking me out."

"Did you fuck him?"

Rose shakes her head. "I've tried but he never had any interest in me. Now I know why."

"Then yes, I forgive you. But I'll tell you this once. If it happens again, I won't hesitate to have you banned." Rose grins from ear to ear and her shoulders sag with relief. "And for the record, I'm not his Ol' Lady."

J. Lynn Lombard

"Not yet anyway," Monica says from behind me.

I shake my head, "Don't you have something to do?" I tease.

"I have someone to do, but they just went into Church." Monica nods her head and I look behind her. Sure enough, all the brothers are piling into Church. Capone is the last one in and his eyes connect with mine. He gives me a wink before disappearing and closing the door behind him.

What I wouldn't give to know what is going on. Capone will tell me when he has a chance if I need to know. My phone has been vibrating in my pocket and I know who it is. Instead of answering it, I turn it off. I have an idea why this happened here tonight and I don't want to be right. I have a feeling it was a message to me for ignoring them. But I'm not going down that road. Not tonight and I hope not ever.

"Monica?" I call out to her. She turns in my direction. "Did we lose anyone tonight?"

Sadness etches in her eyes and she nods her head. "The prospect, Alex, guarding the gates."

"We need to do something for him and the boys before they come out of Church," I suggest.

"What'd you have in mind?"

Capone's Chaos

"A memorial in his honor and dinner ready for them when they come out. They need to eat and we need to feed them."

"I'll help in the kitchen," Rose speaks up.

"So, can I and I'll grab a few girls still here," Daisy says from across the room. "Let me get Kensi and Aerial." She quickly leaves, heading to the back of the Clubhouse where the girls are staying.

Only a few of them remained here after the Royal Bastards rescued them from Bloody Scorpions. We still haven't been able to track Aerial's mom or dad down yet so she's been staying in Daisy's room with her. Once in a while, she will stay with me, but at night, I'm in no shape to have a child with me. My anxiety and stress reach all time high's when night falls and the Clubhouse is quiet. Half the time I'm lucky I make it through the night without clawing my skin off or ripping my hair out. I hope something gives soon because I can't keep going on like this.

A few hours later, the Brother's bellies are full and peace has washed over all of us. Capone stands, gaining the attention of everyone around. His eyes are full of anguish and sorrow, breaking my heart with the pain he's feeling.

"Brothers, we lost a prospect tonight by the hands of the Salazar Cartel." Capone closes his eyes and takes a deep breath. As he opens them, the expression on his face changes from mournful to revenge. His grip tightens on his beer bottle turning his knuckles white. "We will get payback. We will honor Alex's death by killing every single one of those motherfuckers. Some of you know my past with the Salazar Cartel. It's time the rest of you know. You know why this happened and how we'll end this." Fists bang on the tables making the dishes rattle. Several yay's ring out into the clubhouse, echoing across the room. "But first we need to honor a fallen brother."

After Tiny and Dagger fixed the gates, they took care of Alex's body and brought his prospect cut inside and laid it on the bar. Alex had no family that we are aware of, so no one was contacted about his death. Capone walks across the room and grabs Alex's bloody cut. After he brings it back to the table, he rips the prospect patch off with his knife. "Alex, you will always be a part of this club. You sacrificed your life to protect us and in return, we are making you a full-time brother in the afterlife. We'll seek revenge on your death and will not stop until they all suffer. Rest in peace and watch down upon us." Capone holds up Alex's cut with both hands and all the members of RBMC shout Amen. Capone walks over to the wall where there are previous member's cuts hung up and places Alex's on the end.

"Ride hard and give 'em hell, brother." Capone bangs his fist on the wall in three rapid successions. He heads back over and sits in his seat. I bring a fresh beer and place it in front of him. "Thank you." He offers me a panty melting smile before taking a long pull.

Capone's Chaos

"You're welcome." I turn to head back to my seat when Capone's strong fingers wrap around my wrist. I peer into his dark eyes, looking for a sign he is unsure. Once I take this step, there is no going back. Either he's made up his mind and wants to be with me or this is some cruel joke the world is playing on me. Capone tugs me toward him and pulls me down onto his lap. My small frame doesn't take up much space to his large one. His chin rests on my shoulder, his arms around my waist. A shiver races down my spine as his hot breath fans across my skin. He's making a statement in front of everyone and my greedy body is soaking up the meaning of his gesture. I should make him wallow and wait, but damn it, he does things to me where my brain doesn't function and the last thing I want to do is deny him anything. Capone gently kisses my shoulder before his deep voice echoes around the room.

"Back before Chains was dethroned and I took over as President, I found out some information. Only a few of you know about this because it was safer for all involved. Now that the threat has reached our doors, it's time you all know the whole story.

"My mother, as you all know, was born and raised in Mexico. My grandmother was married to Joaquin Salazar, the head of the Salazar Cartel. She too was forced into an arranged marriage. She met my grandfather, Miguel Garcia and became pregnant with my mother. Miguel kept her secret even after the fateful day my grandmother took her last breath.

J. Lynn Lombard

For 20 years, they kept up the affair in secret. Miguel smuggled my mother to the US and arranged for her to marry Chains. It was an arranged marriage to give her safety from the Salazar Cartel. They wanted her back and my grandfather did everything he could to keep her out of their grasp. He even sacrificed his life for her safety. Chains on the other hand had different ideas.

"When my mother became pregnant with me, Chains used that to his advantage to get in with the Salazar Cartel. Thinking he was the father to the prince of the Salazar Cartel. Little did he know, I wasn't. He took our club into the drug running for them. One night in Mexico, we were on a run for them. With the secrets both my grandmother and mother carried, no one knew what was going to happen."

***

We arrived in Salazar territory late into the night. My back was aching from riding all day but I pushed forward itching to get the job done. Blayze is riding next to me in the middle of the pack. Chains wanted to punish me for being smart with him earlier in the day when I challenged him on his decision for this run. I had a gut feeling it's not what he says and I questioned him about it.

So, instead of riding in my normal spot behind him, Chains felt I needed to be in the middle where I hate riding. It's petty and annoying but I did what I was told after my mother begged me not to keep

Capone's Chaos

egging him on. Brake lights flash in front of me and we all slow down, turning into a seedy bar in the middle of nowhere. Three dust-covered pick-up trucks are parked haphazardly around the parking lot. Chains lead us to the front of the bar and parks his bike. The rest of us following suit shutting off our bikes. The surrounding night is deathly quiet.

I pull down my neck gaiter and a sinking feeling rests in the pit of my stomach. "Blayze, something isn't right," I whisper to him swinging my leg off my bike.

"I agree, but what are we going to do?" Blayze whispers back.

"Stay alert and watch each other's six. It's all we can do until we know why we're here."

"Capone, Blayze, you two done gossiping like little bitches so we can get this over with?" Chains grumbles near the front of the bar.

"Yeah Chains, we're right behind you," I answer back. Chains' eyes ping pong around like he's expecting someone or something. Blayze and I walk across the dirt driveway and step onto the rundown porch leading into the bar. It reminds me of an old western movie where the horses are tied to the rail and a shootout could happen at any minute. Only our bikes are the horses and the way Chains is watching me, makes me feel like he's going to shoot me any second.

J. Lynn Lombard

"C'mon, let's not keep them waiting any longer." Chains turns on his heels and walks in the door. I follow behind him with Blayze at my six. The rest of the Royal Bastards following behind him. Once we enter the bar, a barmaid is wiping down the counter with a dirty rag. She's incredibly good looking with a tight blue tank top hugging her huge tits and her long black hair on top of her head in one of those messy bun things.

Tables are scattered apart and six men are sitting in the far back watching us enter. Chains struts over to them and shakes each of their hands.

"Sorry we're late, Sir. It was a bitch passing through customs. Our guy on the inside was called in at the time we were rolling through." Chains answers the unspoken question. Even though that's not what happened at all. We're late because he had to stop in Tijuana to get his dick sucked by one of his many side pieces.

The man in the middle grunts and taps his cigar on the wooden table, even though an ashtray is right in front of him. He's wearing a grey fitted suit that's pressed to perfection. His grey hair is cropped close to his head without a strand out of place even in this heat. He reeks of money and power. He eyes me carefully before nodding to the man sitting next to him. The other guy stands up and motions with his head for Chains to follow.

I start to follow too until Chains stops me. "You stay here. Shooter, with me."

Capone's Chaos

"What the fuck, Chains? This isn't protocol," I growl.

"You'll do as I fucking say. Stay here, get a beer. Maybe take that hot little number in the back. We got this handled."

"Chains, this isn't our protocol," I argue.

"Look kid, I'm not doing this with you. Stay. The. Fuck. Here." Chains punctuates every word pissed off.

"Fine, but I'm not saving your ass when shit goes sideways. You know Shooter is as worthless as your dick in my mother." I turn my back on Chains and walk to the bar with Blayze hot on my heels. Chains disappears in the back room with two of these men, Shooter and two of ours. I sit on the dusty barstool, ignoring everyone around me.

"Give me a Corona," I wink at the barmaid. She doesn't deserve my pissed off attitude. I imagine she deals with enough from this Cartel. Things with Danyella are at a standstill. We're better off as friends right now until she finds what she needs in her life. The barmaid slides my beer into my hands and I go to pay for it.

"It's on the house," she shakes her head at the wad of pesos I pull out.

"Thanks. What's your name?" I ask taking a long pull of my Corona.

J. Lynn Lombard

"Layla. What's yours?" Layla leans on the bar, showing me her ample cleavage. My eyes drift down the V in her tank top before roaming back up. Her skin is glowing with a dark tan and her smoky eyes are full of lust and desire. It's been a while since I've felt the underlying lust between us.

"Capone." There's something about Layla that's attractive. Maybe it's because she's unknown, working in a seedy bar in the middle of nowhere.

"Well, Capone, I could use some help in the back getting some boxes down, if you're strong enough to handle it." Layla looks at me through hooded lashes. "It's been a while since someone strong enough could handle the lift."

I glance at Blayze and he nods his head. He'll watch my back while I'm occupied. "Lead the way, Layla." I let her name roll off my tongue and follow her into the back room.

She takes my hand and the moment we're in the back room with the door closed, I lift her up and pin her against the wall. Layla spreads her legs, wrapping them around my waist, moaning into my ear. I lift her tank top over her head and her tits spring free. She isn't wearing a bra and her nipples are hard. I lean down and capture one nipple into my mouth, sucking on it while my hand kneads the other.

"Dios mio, Papi," Layla pants, rubbing her pussy against my jean covered dick. "Fuck me like you want to."

Capone's Chaos

I release her tit and suck on her neck, not kissing her. I have an unwritten rule I don't kiss those I fuck. I reach down and pop the button of her shorts, my hand diving into her panties, seeing she's soaking wet for me already. I pinch and rub her clit sending her into a fit of Spanish.

I unbuckle and unzip my jeans releasing my hard and aching cock. I grab a condom and roll it on. Keeping Layla pinned against the wall, I surge forward into her hot, wet pussy, driving hard into her, making her scream my name over and over.

Once we're both finished, I dispose of the condom and leave the backroom, letting Layla get herself together. Sated and satisfied, I walk out the front door to get some fresh air. A twinge of remorse hits me and my thoughts immediately turn to Danyella. I shouldn't feel guilty for having a quick fuck when we're just friends. She's the one that put me in that box and there's nothing I can do about it right now. I light up a cigarette and inhale the smoke, calming my nerves. Once I finish my smoke, I head back inside. The man in the suit, which I'm assuming is the head of the Cartel is still sitting in his spot, now sipping on whiskey. His dark eyes are watching my every move. Layla is nowhere in sight. I breathe a sigh of relief.

Chains comes out of the backroom, a wild look in his eyes. Well, motherfucker, he's higher than a fucking kite. This'll be a fun fucking ride home.

"Capone," Chains bellows across the room.

I roll my eyes and head over to him with Blayze following. "Yeah, Prez?"

"Product is good. I need you to load it up and find us a place for the night."

"Are you fucking kidding me, Chains? That's a prospect's job. Not mine." I growl.

"You'll do as I fucking say, boy. I'm the President of this Charter, not you. You're my son and do what the fuck I tell you to do." Chains raises his voice, causing everyone to turn in our direction.

"And I've earned my fucking patch. There is no Prospect on my back." I shout back.

"There's no Prospects here. Do as I fucking say now before you'll regret it."

"Capone," Blayze interrupts our argument with a hand on my shoulder. "Let's just get the shit done and get the fuck out of here."

"Listen to your little follower, Capone." Chains spits out.

He really wants me to deck him in his cock sucking mouth. I can't wait for the day I take that motherfucker to ground. "This isn't over. Not by a long shot." I turn on my heels and go outside. "Mother fucker is asking for it big time. I can't wait for him to get what's coming to him. Who in the fuck does he think he is?" I pace back and forth along the

Capone's Chaos

dirt driveway. The three pick up trucks that were parked around the bar have moved closer, caging our bikes in.

"Boss said you're the one in charge of this." One man says dropping the tailgate. He slides the cover off and inside are several white and brown bricks. How in the fuck am I getting all of these on our bikes and past customs? Releasing a deep sigh, I slide on my riding gloves and load up the cargo. Putting two or three bricks in each saddlebag. We had custom saddlebags made for runs like these. There's a drop down compartment hidden on each bike, but there is more product than what we have room for. Once each bike, including Chains' bike, is loaded, Blayze and I head back inside.

"We're done," I state.

"Good. And a place to stay for the night?" Chains asks.

"I've got a place you can stay at." The man sitting at the table says. He takes a sip of whiskey before nodding his head at Layla. "There is a house down the end of this road." His gaze doesn't leave mine.

"Who are you and why would you offer us a place to stay. What's the catch?" I ask skeptically.

"Joaquin Salazar, head of the Salazar Cartel, Nieto." He takes another sip of whiskey before continuing. "No catch for familia. Consider the offer a

sign of what you call good faith. There is liquor and plenty of cono for all of you." Joaquin answers in broken English.

"Thank you, Senior Salazar. We're grateful for your hospitality," Chains speaks up, offering his hand for Joaquin to shake. I look at Chains with my eyebrows raised. He's never been this polite to anyone. Joaquin shakes his hand and whispers something to Chains I can't hear. Chains nods his head in an answer before turning to all of us. "Load up and ride out. We'll stay here for the night and head out first thing in the morning."

Something else is going on but I haven't figured out what it is yet. I don't like this one bit and I won't be sleeping at all, unlike the other brothers who have no clue something is about to go down.

Capone's Chaos

Chapter 8

Capone

Retelling this part of my past is harder than I thought it would be. We haven't even touched the extra runs I had to make on my own. Or how I was almost thrown in jail in Mexico for messing around with Layla. Or how I found out who Joaquin Salazar really was.

"Capone?" Danyella shifts on my lap, rubbing her ass against my dick. I look down at her, ready to see the hate and confusion in her eyes. It's not there. "I'm not mad or hurt. Continue or you'll never heal."

"How'd you know?"

"Derek, I'm not blind or stupid. I know you've been with other women. It's my fault where our relationship was headed. We were both too young to commit to each other. It's OK. Keep going." Danyella encourages me.

I look around the table and every member of the Royal Bastards MC are watching the two of us, waiting for me to continue. Some are nodding their heads, captivated by my story. I release a deep breath and continue.

"That night, I didn't sleep. Blayze and I stayed with the bikes the whole night, watching over them while Chains and the rest of his loyal members went inside to party and fuck. It made my stomach turn how he disregarded his President position and I knew then something needed to be done. Questions on why we're mixed up with the Cartel plagued me all night long. Answers I never got until the fourth run down there."

***

This is our fourth run down here and each time makes my skin crawl. Layla keeps coming around each time we pull into the bar and meet with Joaquin. Which has been fine with me because while Chains is in the back, she keeps me company in her backroom. Joaquin keeps giving me looks that I can't decipher and I don't like it one bit.

This run is different than the last three. This time it's just Blayze and me riding on the dusty road toward the bar we first went to. We pull up to the doors and park in our normal spot. I remove my Royal Bastards neck gaiter from my mouth and nose and take off my sunglasses. The dust is worse today than before. According to the weather before we left, it said there was a dust storm heading in our direction.

"Let's make this pick up quick and get out of here before the storm hits," I tell Blayze.

Capone's Chaos

"Yeah, I don't like how it's just the two of us today. Stay alert and I'll watch your six." Blayze responds.

"I'll watch yours. Come on, brother. Let's get this over with." Blayze and I knuckle bump before dismounting our bikes and heading inside.

The door slams shut behind us and it takes my eyes a few seconds to adjust to the darkness inside. Layla is at the bar again, wiping it down with the same rag. She doesn't look up and smile at me like she normally does. In fact, she avoids my gaze and leaves the room. That's weird.

Joaquin Salazar is sitting in his normal spot in the booth in the back, sipping on a glass of whiskey. None of his men are around him either. The hair on the back of my neck stands on end and my gut is telling me something's off.

"Let's do this. Get in and out. I'm not liking this." I whisper to Blayze.

"I agree. Something isn't right." Blayze whispers back.

Together we walk across the dirty floor, our boots stomping along the way. I run my fingers through my hair before sitting across from Joaquin.

"You made it, Capone." Joaquin takes another sip of whiskey, his dark eyes don't leave my face.

J. Lynn Lombard

"I didn't really have a choice, Joaquin. Let's get this over with so we can head back before the storm hits." I answer leaning back in my seat.

"Did Chains tell you why I requested only the two of you?"

"No. He doesn't tell me anything."

"Well, he should have so you could be more prepared. What I'm going to tell you is something you might not want to hear, but I'm getting old, Nieto. I need my heir back." Joaquin watches my reaction.

"What the fuck are you talking about?" I raise my eyebrow waiting for his answer.

"Fifty years ago, I married a woman. It was what you'd call an arranged marriage to keep our Cartel strong. There was no love between us, but we had a child, a nina. When my wife became sick, our hija disappeared into thin air. No clues where she went to. Not until recently." Joaquin takes the last sip of his whiskey and holds his glass up for a refill. Layla comes over with a fresh glass and doesn't meet my gaze. That's fine with me because all she really was, was a quick fuck with no emotions attached. "As I was saying, my daughter has recently been found along with her son, my grandson. The male heir to my Cartel. My Nieto."

I process everything he's saying and my heart races in my chest. Does Joaquin think I'm his heir? "That's impossible, Salazar. I can't be your heir."

Capone's Chaos

"Why not, Nieto? Your mother's real name is Elena Salazar. Ask her about it and let me know what she says. Miguel Garcia played his part by keeping my wife, your grandmother, Maria occupied but he betrayed me by taking my daughter. And for that, he paid for with his life."

My heart is racing in my chest and my brain is running a million miles an hour. Salazar killed my grandfather? I abruptly stand and head for the door. Fuck the deal, fuck the drugs, fuck this whole fucking thing. Blayze is right behind me and together we ride off back to the US, looking for answers. Consequences be fucking damned with Chains if what Salazar just told me is true.

***

I'm brought back to the present with warm arms wrapped around my waist and soft curves snuggled against me. My Belle is holding me tight, not caring who sees.

"Wait, isn't your father MadDog and not Chains?" Daisy asks. She's sitting next to Torch, her hand resting on his on the table. She's been around here long enough she knows quite a bit about the club.

"Yes. That's where the danger comes in. Chains thought I was his and tried to play that to his advantage. When Blayze and I got back, I talked to my mother and she finally told me the whole story. How my grandmother Maria had an illegitimate child

J. Lynn Lombard

with Miguel Garcia. Two children actually. My mother Elena and my uncle Reaper. Miguel and Maria were able to keep Reaper a secret by her going away for several months until after the baby was born. Then Miguel left him in the care of an MC in Mexico so Salazar would never find out.

"After Miguel smuggled my mother out of Mexico under the guise of following up on some of the Cartel's dealings, he returned to Mexico and Salazar killed him for his betrayal. I still don't know how Salazar found out about it, but my guess is Chains had something to do with it. Miguel thought he was keeping my mother safe by having her marry Chains. No one thought a prestigious MC such as the Royal Bastards would turn on her. Chains did. Once she confessed these secrets to me, Blayze, Reaper and I moved my mother to a safe house and Monica to Detroit to keep her safe. A year later I brought Chains down for betraying our club. I stripped him of his patch, left him for dead in the middle of the desert and stepped in as President.

"A few months after we hid Elena, I received word that a member of another MC was kicking it in my area, asking questions which would stir up a huge mess if he asked the wrong people. So, Blayze and I went for a ride and tracked him down. He was trying to find my mother. We found them together in her hideout and she confessed her last secret. That this man from Deadly Sins MC, Mt. Pleasant, was MadDog, my biological father. She told me, with proof, how Chains tried to use me to get in with the

Capone's Chaos

Salazar Cartel, thinking I was their heir and he would be rich. How he used the Royal Bastards and owed the Cartel a fuck ton of money for drugs he never sold. Salazar was coming after us for Chains' betrayal."

"What does that have to do with us today? Didn't this happen a few years ago?" Red asks, sitting to the left of me. He's so enraptured in my story, he forgot about the beer sitting in front of him.

"Salazar is done waiting. I was able to smooth talk him to give us time to pay him back, but now the times up. He wants either his money or blood spilled." I hug Danyella tighter to me. Thinking about what he wants in exchange for our debt owed brings a chill down my spine. I haven't even told Blayze what Salazar wants. I'll be damned if I let that happen.

"So, we go in and we end the motherfucker for fucking with our Club." This comes from Torch, who still has a hold of Daisy's hand.

"That's the plan. I need Red to hack into Salazar's compound and find the ins and outs of his operation. Grab someone to help you. Then we take a ride down to Mexico and end his tirade." Hoots and hollers echo around the room with fists banging on the table. "While we're at it, Scorch from the Elizabeth City Chapter has a job for us. He needs some fireworks let off at the Alcazar compound. They fucked with one of ours and we're going to make them pay. Torch, I've already talked to you about it. We'll handle that before we hit Salazar."

"You got it, Prez," Torch's eyes light up with the task. He's in his element when he can blow shit up.

"Well, now you know the whole story about my fucked-up life, let's honor the death of Alex and let loose. We all need it." I rap my knuckles on the dining room table and my brothers follow suit. I hold up my beer and salute Alex. "For Alex, may we ride hard, keep both tires on the asphalt and return home to play harder."

"For Alex!" Cheer ring out as we all take a drink. One of the patch whores crank the music up and everyone disperses from the table heading in different directions.

Blayze, Monica and Danyella stay at the table. Danyella's still on my lap and I don't want her to move. I love the way she's pressed against me. Her soft curves molding to my body. The way her scent flutters across my nose, teasing me.

"Capone, what is it you're not telling everyone else?" Blayze asks.

"I've told you everything."

"Are you sure you're not leaving something out?"

Capone's Chaos

"Positive. Salazar needs to be dealt with immediately. The sooner the better before he comes here and wants blood." Blayze watches me carefully before taking Monica's hand and they take off toward his room, leaving Danyella and me alone.

"About time I get you all to myself," Danyella says, gripping my face and pulling it down to hers. She presses a soft kiss to my lips pulling away before I can deepen the kiss. "Come on, I want to show you something."

The spark in her eyes has me up and following her in a heartbeat. She grips my hand, pulling me along with her until we're at the door to my bedroom. I raise my eyebrows at her as Danyella unlocks and opens the door. She leads me inside and pushes me down onto my bed.

"I'm a little nervous, but this is the way I wanted your welcome home to go. After our texts last night, I decided to say fuck it and go for what I want." Danyella stands between my open legs.

I wrap my arms around her waist, pulling her closer to me. "What is it you want, my Belle?" My voice is husky with need. I want this woman more than I've ever wanted someone in my life. I want her under me, over me, beside me for the rest of our lives. I'm done fighting my feelings for her.

Danyella grips my face and brings her lips inches from mine. "You Derek. I want you." Her breath fans across my face, sending my body into overdrive. "But I need to know if you want this too. Once we take this next step, there is no going back. There are no surprises or secrets between us anymore. No one but me warms your bed or takes this cock."

"Belle," I grip Danyella's hips tighter, pulling her against me. "You're all I've ever wanted or needed." I look up and into her eyes. Her lashes are hooded over the beautiful emeralds. Danyella's breath hitches in her throat. "No one has even touched this cock in a long time besides my hand and that's from thinking about you."

Her lips crash onto mine and I plunge my tongue inside Danyella's mouth. She moans and grips the back of my hair, pulling us closer together. We're a frenzy of lips and tongues battling back and forth. I lean back onto the bed, pulling Danyella over top of me. Her legs are straddling my hips, her pussy grinding onto my aching cock begging for relief. Moans and groans fill the room and I buck up into her, rubbing my hardness along her covered pussy.

I yank Danyella's shirt and bra over her head, revealing her tits. "Fuck, you're perfect." My mouth closes around one nipple while I tease the other with my hand. Her hips grind down harder and a moan escapes her throat.

"Fuck, Derek. I need you," Danyella pants. Her hips are bucking wildly, driving me crazy with need and want. I suck on her pebbled nipple one last time before popping it out of my mouth and attacking the other one. "Oh, God."

I flip us over so she's underneath me. I kiss my way down her stomach until I reach the button of her shorts. I look up at Danyella and she nods her head. I unbutton her shorts and drag them down her legs along with her panties so she's bare in front of me. Her pussy shining with her juices. I shrug out of my cut and lay it on my dresser. I toe off my boots, toss my t-shirt and jeans haphazardly onto the pile of our clothes on the floor. Danyella is watching me with her legs spread apart, no shyness or second guessing this is what she wants. She wants me and I will give her anything she desires.

I climb my way onto the bed until my face is at the apex of her thighs, inhaling her succulent scent.

"Derek, I'm losing my mind," Danyella pleads.

"Belle, I'm going to rock your fucking world." I stare into her eyes. "Are you sure about this? Once we go here, there's no turning back."

"Derek, I'm more than sure. I've been sure of us for a long time. I was an idiot for making us wait." She whispers.

I can't hold back any longer. I need to taste her on my tongue. I drag my tongue along the seam of her hip toward her swollen clit. I lick and suck along her perfect pussy, tasting her delicious flavor on my tongue. Danyella grips my head, holding me to her as I feast on her beautiful body. She moans as I drag a finger along her opening and plunge it inside while I lick and suck on her clit driving her wild with need.

"Oh, God," Danyella moans.

"There is no God here, Belle, only me." My cock is so hard, I could punch through a steel wall. But I tamp it down for a moment because the only thing that matters right now is Danyella and her pleasure. My fingers are working her pussy as my mouth attacks her clit, driving her to the brink.

"I'm coming, Derek. Oh God, I'm coming," Danyella pants tightening her grip on my hair.

I keep working her body to my pleasure as her pussy clamps down on my fingers and her hips buck into my face. She moans my name in ecstasy as she falls over the edge of bliss. Once her breathing comes back to normal, I release my hold on her and kiss my way up her body until we're face to face.

"I'm not done with you yet, Belle." I grind my hard cock onto her pussy and Danyella responds by bucking up into me.

"I'm ready, Derek. So ready."

I strip my boxers off and grab a condom off my dresser. Before I can put it on, Danyella is on her knees at the edge of the bed. She's staring at my swollen cock with passion.

Capone's Chaos

"You want a taste, Belle?" Danyella nods her head and what can I say, I'm a sucker to give her anything she wants. She lowers herself so her mouth is level with my cock and pulls me into her mouth. The moment her lips wrap around my cock, I'm a goner. She sucks me inside and moans, vibrating around my dick. Danyella does this a handful of times and my eyes roll in the back of my head. "Fuck, Belle. That feels perfect." Danyella sucks me into her mouth harder and I swear my eyes cross. My heart beats hard against my chest and tingles work their way from my toes up into my balls. I pull her off me and bring her face up next to mine. We're both breathing hard.

"You're the most beautiful woman I've ever had." I kiss Danyella hard before laying her down and covering her with my body. Danyella spreads her legs, making room for me. I kiss her again. "Are you ready, Belle?"

"God, Derek, I'm ready. I've been ready. Fuck me like you need." Danyella pants.

Sitting up, I roll the condom on and line up my cock to her pussy, feeling the warmth of her wrapping around me. Inching in, I wait a few seconds, not only to get myself under control but to let her adjust to my size. Once Danyella shifts to pull me closer, I surge into her pussy, moaning her name. I thrust in and out, slow at first then pick up the pace and Danyella meets me thrust for perfect thrust. I lean down to suck one nipple into my mouth and Danyella goes wild scratching my back with her nails.

"Derek," my name rolling off her lips drives me crazy.

"Belle, fuck me, Belle." I can tell I'm close. I drive in harder on each thrust, hitting her clit with my groin. Her pussy tightens around my shaft and she's panting and moaning. She wraps her legs around my waist, her tits bouncing with every thrust. I slow my movements for a moment and pull out. Sitting back, I pull Danyella with me. She straddles my hips and sinks back down onto my cock. This angle lets me get deeper inside of her and gives her some control. "Ride my cock, Belle. Take it all."

"Fuck, Derek." Danyella sinks onto my cock over and over, her pussy squeezing me with all her strength. Her chest is heaving and I suck one tit into my mouth. "Oh, shit Derek. I'm coming. Keep doing that." So I do. I suck one nipple hard, leaving my mark on her. She rides my cock until I'm seeing stars and my skin tingles.

"I'm coming, Belle. Don't stop." Danyella doesn't. She slams her pussy onto my cock until I explode. "Fuck me." I pull her close and surge into her one last time. My orgasm shoots through me hard and fast at the same time she explodes around me, tightening onto my shaft. We're a mess of kisses and heavy breathing while we both come back down. My dick twitches, emptying everything I have left.

Capone's Chaos

I lay back on the bed and pull Danyella with me while we both catch our breaths. With her head on my chest, Danyella's tracing the tattoos up and down my arm with light feathery touches. Something's on her mind and I patiently wait for her to tell me what it is.

Danyella lifts her head and looks me in the eyes. "What's on your mind, Belle?"

"Nothing."

"Don't tell me nothing. I can see it on your face. Somethings bothering you and I want to know what it is." I kiss her forehead, giving her courage to say what she's thinking.

"You're going to think I'm nuts."

"Try me."

"I want to go to Mexico with you. Me and Monica both. I just got you and she just married my brother. I don't want to be apart from you right now." She's pleading for me to give in with her succulent green eyes but I can't. She's in more danger than she knows about. "See you think it's nuts."

"Yes, it is. We're not going there on a vacation." Danyella huffs and gets off the bed. She's pissed off. "Danyella, wait."

"No, you wait, Derek. I told you I didn't want to say and now you know why. You think I'm nuts."

J. Lynn Lombard

She stomps into the attached bathroom and slams the door.

Huffing, I climb off the bed and go after her. I open the bathroom door and she's sitting on the floor, her legs drawn up into her chest, her arms wrapped around her legs. "Belle, I don't think you're nuts. I think the idea is nuts."

"Why? Why is it nuts? Because I want to be with you? Because I'll cramp your style? Why can't I go?" She's shouting and upset and it's pissing me off I've upset her.

"Danyella, it's not safe for you."

"Why isn't it safe? What are you hiding?" I don't answer because I know if I do, I'll spill everything to her. "You're hoping to see this Layla chick again, aren't you? You got what you wanted from me and now you want her again."

"No! I'm not going there to see her again. Where in the fuck is all of this coming from?" My jaw starts ticking, now I'm really pissed the fuck off.

"Then what the fuck is the big deal?" We're both shouting and she's ignoring my question. I'm so confused about how we went from a blissful night to yelling and arguing. I have to tell her why she shouldn't go with me or she'll keep thinking the worst.

Capone's Chaos

"We're going there to protect the Club." Danyella rolls her eyes. "If you go with me, I can't protect you."

"That doesn't make any sense, Capone." She spits out my road name in disgust. "I don't need protection." Danyella stands up and goes back into the bedroom. "Quit telling me lies."

Danyella grabs her shirt off the floor and yanks it over her head. She finds her panties and jabs her legs into them.

"I'm not lying, Belle. Not about this."

"Bullshit. I can tell you're hiding something. I'm not dumb nor am I stupid. You don't want me to go so you can have a quick fuck with your side piece."

I grab her arm and pull her into me. "I swear I haven't touched her years. And I don't want to. You're the only one I want. I'm not like Chains or your father at all."

"Then why can't I go?" She sobs into my chest.

"It's not safe for you, Belle."

"That's not good enough, Derek. Tell me why you don't want me to go."

"I want you to go. I want to spend every minute with you. But it's not safe." I pull her head off my chest so I can look into her eyes. "Salazar wants to take you and I'll be damned if I let that happen. If you go with me, I can't keep you protected."

"What?" She sucks in a deep breath.

"It's one thing I haven't even told your brother yet. Salazar has his sights set on you. Said if I don't pay him back for Chains' fuck up, he's coming after you." I confess. "That's why I can't let you go with me. That's why I need you to stay here where I know you're safe."

"All you had to do was tell me this. If I knew my life was in danger last time, I would've been more careful and I never would've been taken by the Bloody Scorpions. Keeping things like this from me is dangerous, not only to you but to me too."

"I know this now. Damn you're hot when you're mad." Danyella slaps my chest. "But I'm serious about this. It's more dangerous if you go with us than if you stay here."

"Ok. I'll stay but under extreme protest. And if that bitch comes anywhere near you, I will cut off her tits and shove them up her ass." Danyella's threat turns me on.

"I wouldn't expect anything less from you." I kiss her briefly on the lips. "We're good now?"

"Yeah, we're good. I'm sorry I freaked. I don't know what's wrong with me."

Capone's Chaos

"There's nothing wrong with you. You're perfect the way you are, Belle." I kiss her again and she melts from my touch. I need to make sure she knows she's the one I want. The one I need.

"I'm fucked in the head, Derek. It's something I have to work on, on my own. I should be trusting you, but instead, I think the worst. I don't know why and it annoys the hell out of me." Danyella confesses and it breaks my heart.

"Belle, I get it. It just means I have to show you no matter where I am or what I'm doing, you're the one I want." I pick her up and she wraps her legs around my waist, her arms around my neck. I prove to her all night long she's the only woman on my mind.

J. Lynn Lombard

Chapter 9

Capone

Sunlight streaming into my bedroom window awakens me. Blayze and I are the only two members who have rooms on the outer walls of our Clubhouse. The rest of the rooms are deep inside. This way we can protect our club and the people inside.

Danyella's naked body is wrapped around mine, sound asleep. Her leg is draped over my waist, her pussy I've been inside numerous times last night is near my growing cock and her head is resting on my chest. Her breaths are deep and even. I have to get up and ready to hit the road but I don't want to leave the comfort of Belle's arms. I've finally got her right where I've wanted her for years and I have to leave her. It's one of the hardest things I've had to do in a long time. This doesn't compare to hiding my mother away and not seeing her for her safety. Danyella has me wrapped around her finger and she's embedded into my heart.

I kiss the top of her head and she wiggles closer to me. Her pussy is dangerously close to my aching cock, begging to get inside of her one more time. I run my fingers lightly up and down her back. My other hand sneaks down to her pussy and I finger her clit. She's soaking wet for me while she's asleep. Danyella arches her hips into my hand and a whimper escapes her plump lips that are swollen from kissing them all night. She tilts her face up to me and slowly opens her eyes. I don't stop fingering her clit. I stroke the swollen nub a little faster. I drag her hot body over mine so her pussy is resting on my cock. I don't slip inside yet. Danyella lifts herself up and places gentle kisses along my jaw while rubbing herself along the length of my shaft. A moan escapes my throat and she bucks her hips into me harder. I swear I'm going to come all over myself if she keeps this up. Danyella shifts just right and my cock slips inside her pussy, her walls clamping around me.

A moan escapes both our lips at the same time. "Fuck, Belle."

She rides my cock, slowly raising her hips and pushing back down again. I grab her hips and push up into her at the same time she comes down. We do this repeatedly, making love slowly and tenderly. I kiss her hard plunging my tongue inside her mouth. I grunt and she moans as she rides my cock.

"Shit, Derek. I'm going to come." Danyella shifts so her legs are at my waist and sits up, sinking down further onto me. I strum her clit with my fingers, bringing her closer to the edge, watching our bodies slap together. My spine tingles, signaling I'm close too.

"Keep going, Belle. I'm close," I encourage her. Together we shatter into a million pieces as we come apart for each other and my heart surrenders to her willingly. Those three little words want to pass through my lips, but I hold them in as I ride the wave of ecstasy with the one I'm meant to be with. The one who has always been apart of me.

Danyella and I take a quick shower, well, as quick as it can be when this woman makes me rock hard just by breathing. Now we're dressed and heading to the kitchen with my arm around her neck and hers around my waist. The kitchen is full of brothers getting around to start our long ride. Torch is sitting at the table nestled in the corner drinking a cup of coffee, Daisy is next to him eating. Those two have become pretty close since she recovered from her gunshot wound. She still carries the scars from that night both mentally and physically, but Torch has helped her get past a lot of what happened to her.

Trigger, Red, Bear and Dagger are fucking around at the island and didn't hear us enter. Those four act like a bunch of college boys with all the bullshit and jokes they play on each other.

"Morning, Prez. Danyella. Don't use the sugar," Bear sulks.

"I'm not even going to ask," I respond.

Capone's Chaos

Red, Dagger and Trigger are trying to hold in their laughter at a sulking Bear. "These fuckers thought it would be funny to replace the sugar with salt." Bear chokes down a swallow of his coffee. "It wasn't funny, fuckers." The three of them lose it and start laughing. Bear throws something at them and before I know it, there is an all out food fight happening in the kitchen.

I hurry past them, leaving Danyella by Torch and Daisy and grab some food before they decide to use it all. Making two quick plates of breakfast, I settle down next to Danyella and we eat. Dagger and Bear team up against Red and Trigger. I let them get their fun out now because what we're going into won't be very fun. I'll have the patch whores clean up their mess.

"Boys!" I shout over their antics. The four of them stop what they're doing and face me covered in food. "We leave in twenty. Be ready to go."

Dagger and Red leave the kitchen and Trigger and Bear follow shortly after. Blayze and Monica come into the room and see the mess they made. Blayze shakes his head, steps over the food on the floor and fixes himself and Monica a plate. Monica leaves the kitchen really quick and comes back by the time Blayze has their plates at the table next to the four of us.

J. Lynn Lombard

"Rose and a few other girls will be in shortly to clean this up," Monica says. Danyella stiffens at the mention of Rose. That's weird.

"Belle, what's wrong?" I ask.

"Nothing, why?"

"You're acting weird."

"No, I'm not. I'm eating." She shoves a fork full of food into her mouth. I drop it. She'll tell me when she's ready. But if Rose has done anything to make Danyella uncomfortable, I will banish her from the Clubhouse.

"Blayze, Torch, we're leaving soon. Are you guys ready? I want to get down there before nightfall." I'm apprehensive about leaving, but we need to do it.

"Yeah, Prez. As soon as I'm done eating I'll be ready to go." Torch says.

"Good. Take only what you need, Scorch will have all you need waiting for you down there. That way we don't get caught crossing the border with any evidence."

"Got it, Prez. It's going to be a show for sure." Torch rubs his hands together with a glint in his eyes. He's in his element when he can blow shit up. It's how he got his road name, Torch.

Danyella and I finish eating and she takes our plates to the sink. Her shoulders are slumped like the weight of the world is resting on them. I approach her from behind and wrap my arms around her waist.

"It's going to be OK, Belle. I promise. You have protection here."

Danyella inhales a deep breath before straightening her shoulders. "I know. It's harder than what I thought it would be. When I used to watch Monica tell you guys goodbye I was jealous she got to do it and I didn't. Now that I can, I don't want too. I don't want my heart to ride away." She turns in my arms and rests her head on my chest.

"If it makes you feel any better, my heart will be here and I'll take yours with me." Danyella looks up at me and blinks. I give her my best smile, the one she loves to see.

"What?"

"You heard me." I kiss the tip of her nose. "Your heart will go with me and I'll leave mine here for you." A smile graces her lips and she stands on her tiptoes to meet my lips. We kiss long and slow, not giving a fuck who's around.

"Take that shit elsewhere. The last thing I want burned in my brain is my baby sister's tongue shoved down my Presidents throat." Blayze mumbles. I hear a slap and a grunt and break our kiss, resting my forehead against Danyella's.

"I have to go." I exhale.

"I know. Come on, I'll see you out."

Together we walk hand in hand toward the garage. Everyone is out here, loading up to ride off. Red, Dagger and their prospects are staying behind to keep an eye on the girls and keep them safe. I walk over to my Harley and pull Danyella with me. She will get the chance to give me a proper goodbye this time. Daisy is with Torch and Monica is with Blayze. Her tongue is already shoved down his throat. Something I've gotten used to since they made it official. I should be pissed, but now that I have Danyella, I see why their goodbyes were always that way.

I straddle my bike and put my half helmet on. Danyella is standing next to me unsure what to do. I strap on my gloves and pull her against me. She's holding back tears, making her green eyes shine.

"Don't cry, Belle. I'll be back before you know it. Remember my heart is with you." I kiss her hard and passionately before breaking away. "You have my number, call or text when you need me. I'll let you know when we get there."

"Ride safe and keep the tires on the asphalt." Danyella backs up until she's standing next to Monica and Daisy.

"Always. Don't get into trouble while we're gone." I point at Monica and she giggles.

Capone's Chaos

"We'll be good. I promise." Monica's promise doesn't reassure me like it should but I can't worry about that right now. That sister of mine knows how to get into trouble without even trying.

"Let's roll." I fire up my bike and the rest of my brothers do the same. Together we ride out of the garage in formation. Blayze at my nine, Tiny at my three. Followed by Torch, Derange and Bear. We roll up to the gates and they buzz before opening. The five of us ride out onto the freeway, ready to get down to Mexico and end these fuckers before shit gets too deep

Several hours later, my Harley rumbles down the paved road leading to the Alcazar compound. We park a mile outside the gates and Torch heads inside. I don't ask him what he does or how he does it. This is his element. Blowing shit up and enjoying the chaos that ensues after. We wait for an hour when Torch comes rolling back down the road with a grin on his rugged face.

"It's done, Prez. Send the message to Scorch."

I look behind him with a raised brow and pull out my phone. Just as I hit send, the whole compound lights up like the Fourth of July. I snap a picture and send it to Scorch.

"Let's roll," I put my phone away and fire up my Harley.

J. Lynn Lombard

A few hours later we're riding down the road leading to the bar where I used to meet Salazar. Traveling down to Mexico is all too familiar, even though I haven't been down here in almost six years. I pull up to the rundown porch that leads inside the bar and put my kickstand down. The doors and windows are boarded up and it looks like it hasn't been used in years. I remove my helmet and pull my neck gaiter down.

"Blayze, with me. The rest of you keep a watch out here. This isn't right." I dismount my bike and stroll up the wooden steps. I grab the board across the door and pull it off. The old wood moving easily. I try the knob and it doesn't budge. Blayze and I shoulder the door open and the musty smell of being closed up for so long and the stale liquor assaults my nose making my stomach queasy.

"What the fuck is going on?" Blayze asks. I remove my sunglasses and look around. We're standing in a pile of dust, debris and dried alcohol. No one is here or has been here in years.

"Let's do a sweep just to make sure no one's here." I pull my Glock out of its holster and check the clip. Racking one in the chamber, Blayze and I walk further into the bar. Tables are turned over, chairs are broken and the leather booths are ripped to shreds.

"You check the back room where Chains met with Salazar. I'll check the stock room." Blayze and I part ways and I take a careful step around the bar.

Capone's Chaos

Behind it, smashed bottles litter the floor staining it with dried liquor and what looks like blood. I step into the stock room and this room is just as destroyed. Not one box left untouched. Someone vandalized this place and I don't know why. Once I clear the room I meet Blayze back out front near the door.

"It's clear. Some dried blood on the other side of the bar but other than that, this place is destroyed."

"Same here. Some blood in the back but no one is here. Capone, what the hell is going on?" Blayze asks.

"I don't know. Let's go to the house Salazar used to set us up in. See if we get any answers there." I put my sunglasses on and step out into fresh air. Torch, Bear, Trigger, Derange and Tiny are waiting next to or on their bikes, watching the area around us. Their heads turn in our direction the moment we're out the door.

"Nothing but destruction in there. We're heading to the house Salazar used to let us use when Chains didn't want to head back." I inform them.

I walk to my bike, put my helmet on and fire it up. The rest of my brothers do the same and we ride to the house. This place like the bar looks abandoned. No one around, not even a creature scurrying past us on the road. I don't know what's going on.

J. Lynn Lombard

    I pull my bike up to the front of the rundown house and put my kickstand down. The rumble from our motors should catch someone's attention. It's not like we're quiet or anything. I watch the windows and doors, waiting for some movement inside but nothing happens.

    "Blayze, Torch and Tiny with me. The rest of you stay out here and be on your guard. Something isn't sitting right with me." I dismount my bike and make my way up to the door. Blayze, Torch and Tiny following close behind. I reach for the doorknob and twist, it gives away easily. I unholster my Glock and we enter the room. This place is abandoned just like the bar and it's hot as hell in here.

    "Torch and I will take the upstairs, Blayze and Tiny search down here. Leaving nothing unturned." I make my way up the creaking stairs, taking them carefully one at a time. Sweat dripping from my forehead, I scan the area above us waiting for some movement. Once we reach the top of the stairs, I enter the room to the left, Torch enters the room to the right. We search each of the six rooms carefully, looking for some kind of clue as to what happened here but come up empty.

    Walking down the stairs, I meet Blayze at the bottom. He's sweating just as badly, shaking his head and defeat wracks my body. What the fuck is happening here?

    "Prez, I don't get it." Blayze wipes the sweat off him. "Something isn't right."

Capone's Chaos

"I know, Blayze. With the Cartel being as powerful as they are, this doesn't make sense." I pace back and forth in the living room.

"Prez, would there be any other place they'd go? It doesn't seem like they'd up and vanish. Is there a compound nearby?" Torch suggests.

"There is one around twenty miles from here but I've never been there. We always met here." I stop pacing and stare out the dirty window. A dreadful feeling setting deep in my stomach. "I'm going to call Red and see how things are there. If it's good, we'll ride down and see if that place is just as dead. I can't shake this feeling." I pull my phone from my cut and dial Red's number. He answers on the second ring.

"Prez."

"Red, how's it going there?"

"All quiet so far. Danyella and Monica are in the gym, the other girls are sitting idle and no one has called or showed up."

"Is someone with them?"

"With who?" Red asks.

I grind my teeth together in annoyance. "Danyella and Monica. Is someone with them?" I growl.

"They're in the gym, Prez. No one has been in or out of here since you guys left." I hear the backdoor open and close. "I'm checking on them now." His heavy boots scuff along the pavement.

My jaw ticks as I hear a door creak open and music comes blaring through the phone. "Danyella! Monica!" The music turns down. "Here, Prez."

"Hello?" Danyella's sexy voice comes across the line.

"Belle, what are you doing?" I turn my back on my brothers to talk to her.

"Monica and I are working out. What are you doing?" I hear the teasing in her voice and it's driving me crazy with need.

"Walking through a dirty, abandoned bar and safe house while sweating my nuts off. Needing to take a shower after being in here."

"Hmm… I'd love to wash the dirt off you. I could wash other things too. You know, to make sure they didn't sweat off." I hear a gagging noise in the background.

"So gross, Danyella! That's my brother you're talking too." Monica shouts.

"Not as bad as hearing you and Blayze. At least I can censor myself and not have phone sex with your brother." Monica grumbles something in the background and Danyella giggles. "Now that she's distracted, tell me what's going on."

Capone's Chaos

Blayze's phone rings in his cut and I lift a brow at him. He shrugs his shoulders and pulls it out. "Hey, beautiful." He walks into the kitchen separating him from us.

"I wanted to check on you and make sure everything is good there," I say to Danyella.

"Yup, everything is good here. Getting in a workout and later Monica and I are going to binge Netflix with Daisy and Aerial." She sounds pretty cheerful and happy.

"Ok, Belle. Have fun and I should be back soon. Put Red back on the phone."

"Stay safe and I'll see you soon. I miss you."

"Miss you too."

"Red!" Danyella shouts. I hear the phone being exchanged.

"Prez," Red says when he gets back on the line.

"Need you at the computer. Put your Prospect on the girls at all times. I don't give a fuck if they're in their rooms. They stand guard and know where they are at all times." I bark into the phone.

"Got it, Prez. Heading to the computers now. Anything you need me to check specifically?" He hurries into the Clubhouse and tells the prospect to stay on the girls at all times. I hear his keys jingle and a door opening. "Ok, Prez, I'm here. What am I looking for?"

"Bring up the bar and the safe house where we're at right now. You can find me on GPS tracking."

I hear the clicking of keys and Red is humming to himself. "Gotcha." He gives a low whistle. "That place is a ghost town."

"No shit, Sherlock. Now span out about twenty miles south of us and tell me what you see."

"Ok, just a sec." I hear clicking again before Red releases another low whistle. "What the fuck happened here?"

"What do you see?"

"Give me a sec, Prez. I want to look around." Red answers. The clicking of keys can be heard through the phone, driving me nuts. "Two days ago, there was activity. Now, there's nothing here, Prez. The compound about twenty miles south of you is deserted. No one coming or going and no one inside. What the fuck's going on?"

"I don't know but you confirmed what I suspected. We're going down there to see if anything is left behind and then heading back. I'll text you when we're on our way."

"Ok, Prez. I'll leave these monitors up and keep watching just in case someone comes before you're there."

Capone's Chaos

"Sounds like a plan. Thanks, Red." I hang up the phone and look around. "Where's Blayze?"

"Still on the phone with your sister." Torch teases.

"Go get him." Torch leaves the room and comes back a few moments later with Blayze hot on his heels.

"Red did a search and the Compound Salazar was in is abandoned, just like these places are. We're riding down there, doing a search then heading back. Let's roll before it gets too late and we're forced to stay the night down here."

"Any idea why he'd leave here?" Blayze asks.

I shake my head. "Not a clue. This was supposed to be a strong cartel but something happened and I don't know what. That's what I'm hoping to find when we get there."

I walk out of the front door and put my sunglasses on. The dry heat blasts me in the face but it feels better than being in the stuffy hotbox of a house. I straddle my bike and the rest of my brothers do the same. Together we ride off toward Salazar's compound, hoping and praying we find something, anything to tell us why he'd abandon this place.

I rub my palm over my chest as a dreadful feeling takes hold deep in my stomach. I need to figure out where he is and why he left before he reaches Danyella.

J. Lynn Lombard

    A horn blaring from my left pulls my attention away from the road in front of me. Before I know it, I'm sailing through the air, my bike skidding behind me. Fuck me. I brace myself for the fall and the pain that'll follow.

Capone's Chaos

Chapter 10

Danyella

I hand the phone back to Red and search out where Monica went too. I find her giggling on the phone, pacing back and forth in the backroom. Instead of eavesdropping on her conversation, I head to the treadmill and set my pace to run while I wait. I pop my earbuds in and begin running, thinking about everything that's happened to me in the past year and the secrets I've been keeping.

I'm so much stronger than I was after Monica rescued me from the Bloody Scorpions. I'm still dealing with the aftermath of the torture I was put through but killing Dred in Michigan helped heal those wounds. Knowing he will never be able to touch me again. No man will ever take anything like that from me ever again.

Taking that next step with Capone was the best outcome I could ask for. He's caring, sweet and gentle with me. I have no remorse or fear when it comes to him touching me. I want it, I crave it. I need it. He's helped me get past my fears and insecurities and I didn't even realize it. Him always being here for me when I need him the most is what's helped me.

Now, I have two choices to make. I can either tell him about what I know and how Salazar is blackmailing me or I can keep it to myself and figure my own way out. I don't know which way to go or how to do it. If I tell him, I risk losing everything we've worked for. If I don't, I risk losing his trust. God, why am I put in this predicament? It's enough to drive a person crazy.

"Danyella, you ready?" Monica asks from behind me, making me jump.

"Holy shit you're a freaking ninja, sneaking up on me like that." I slow the treadmill down and hop off. My heart is still slamming in my chest and I take a deep breath to calm it down.

"I wasn't quiet, you're just lost in your head. Want to talk about it?"

I cut my gaze to the prospect standing at the door and shake my head. "Not here."

Monica nods her head and loops her arm through mine. "Let's get cleaned up and ready for the Netflix marathon."

We leave the gym with the prospect hot on our heels. I turn to him with a raised brow. "Is there a reason you're following us?"

Capone's Chaos

His cheeks turn pink with embarrassment. "I was told by Red to keep an eye on you two at all times."

I roll my eyes, "We're going to shower and watch some hot football players on Netflix. Is that something you're into? Hot men getting all sweaty?" I'm teasing him, but I need him to back off so I can talk to Monica in private.

He yanks on his cut and clears his throat. "Ma'am? I'm sorry did you ask if I were gay?" He fidgets with his cut some more, not looking in our direction.

"It's OK if you are. No judgement from us." I bat my eyelashes and give him an innocent look I've perfected over the years.

The moment he realizes what I'm doing is priceless. "I'm not gay and no I don't want to watch sweaty men play football. I'd rather watch some bikers blow shit up."

"Oh! That reminds me." Monica interrupts our banter. "There's a new show about bikers on Netflix I've been wanting to watch."

"After we watch football, we can get you your biker fix. Deal?"

"Deal." Monica and I walk into the Clubhouse together and the prospect backs off a little, giving me some breathing room. I love Capone for watching out for me, but sometimes a girl just needs girl time. My steps falter at the thought, yanking Monica.

"Danyella, what the...?" She turns around to look at me and a smile forms on her lips. "You just figuring this out now?"

"What? I don't know what you're talking about." I try to shake her off the trail but it isn't working.

"Uh, huh. Bullshit, Belle. I see that look in your eyes." She pulls me into her room and shuts the door. "You just figured out you love Derek."

"Is it that obvious? I mean we just got together, isn't it kind of fast?" My head is running a million miles an hour.

"Girl, you know better than I do how love works." Monica plops on her bed. "He's been after you, trying to get you for years. It's inevitable you fall in love with him."

"But what if he doesn't love me?" I question.

"He does. No man would do what he's done if he doesn't love his woman. Blayze tried to fight it too, but after my attack, that stopped. He realized we're better together than apart and he realized he was the only one who could stop the nightmares." Monica runs her hands down her arms and her palms splay across her stomach. Seeing the pain on her face from losing the one thing she's ever wanted breaks

Capone's Chaos

my heart. "Now, are you going to tell me what you couldn't in the gym?"

I hesitate to answer. I do need to tell someone before shit hits the fan though. I can't keep this inside of me any longer and I need advice on how to move forward. Taking a deep breath, I open my mouth and the words come tumbling out. "Salazar has been trying to blackmail me. He contacted me about a week after you rescued me, telling me if I don't comply with what he wants, he'll kill me, then come after Derek. I don't know what to do or how to tell Derek."

"What the fuck?" Monica's jaw drops and she's speechless.

"Monica, please. I need your help. I don't know what to do." I wring my hands together repeatedly, trying to soothe the pain in my soul.

"What has he asked you to do?"

"Nothing yet. He just keeps texting me, telling me my time is almost up. I'm scared, Monica. I don't know how he found me or what he'll do." I didn't tell her about the last text message. If I did she'd go ballistic. I can't bring that much turmoil to her. Besides, Derek is safe right now. I just talked to him. I don't need to add to Monica's stress.

"Here's what we're going to do. First, you're not leaving my sight. We will both shower in here and you're staying with me tonight. Then, I'll call Capone telling him he needs to come home right away. It's your life in danger, we can't wait until they get back. We need them here now." Monica is acting with a clear head and I'm a mess of confusion.

"I can't sleep in here with you." I shake my head back and forth.

"You don't have a choice, Danyella. You are not leaving my sight for a moment." Monica rises from the bed. "Let's get you a clean change of clothes and some food. It's going to be a long night."

"You don't get it. I can't stay here." I plead. "I can't sleep. I don't sleep. Last night was the first time in over a year I did sleep all night without the nightmares plaguing me. I can't put you in that situation." Tears swell up in my eyes and I take a deep breath.

"Danyella, trust me." Monica puts her hands on my shoulders, comforting. "You're not putting me in any situation. If anyone understands nightmares, it's me. I've been having them since the attack in Detroit. I've been having them since Chains and Steam stabbed and beat me within an inch of my life. I get it and I will help you through them tonight. We will tackle this together."

"Are you sure?" Hope blooms in my chest.

"Positive. I'm not going anywhere and neither are you. You're not alone anymore. You have

Capone's Chaos

me, Blayze and Capone. You have a whole MC that will lay their lives on the line to protect you."

Tears rapidly fall down my cheeks and I take a deep breath, nodding my head. Wiping my face, I stand taller taking the strength Monica is giving me. "OK. But I want to be the one to tell Capone."

Together we walk out of her bedroom and into mine. I quickly gather some clothes for the night and we head into the kitchen. Rose is at the stove cooking something that smells wonderful. Aerial and Daisy are sitting at the island playing a game of cards. Red, Derange and their two prospects come into the kitchen behind Monica and me.

"That's smells delicious, Rose. What are you making?" I ask trying to peek over her shoulder. It's time to bury the past and move forward. I need all the allies I can get at this point.

"Thank you, Danyella. I'm making my famous chicken stir fry." There's a slight accent in her voice I've never heard before and it raises questions in my head.

"Where are you from?" I ask.

"What do you mean? I'm from Los Angeles." The southern accent is gone.

"No, I've heard it a few times, you're accent is from somewhere else. As a matter of fact, I know nothing about you besides what you've shown me. Where are you from originally?" I cross my arms over my chest and lean against the counter next to Rose. I don't think she'll hurt me or anything, I'm curious.

"Danyella, leave it be." Red mumbles from across the room.

I level him with a glare. "With everything going on, I have a right to know where she's from. Don't try to shush me, Red."

He abruptly stands, sending his chair back against the wall. "I said leave it be." Red bellows across the room.

"It's OK, Red. She has a right to know," Rose speaks softly. "Thank you for standing up for me, but I can't hide anymore." Red sits back down with fire in his eyes. Rose sets her spoon down and turns toward me. "I'm from Texas, born and raised. I came to L.A. to escape my past and ended up here with the Royal Bastards."

"Are you hiding from someone?" My heart breaks for this woman in front of me when I see the pain in her eyes.

"Something, not someone. Not anymore." Rose shakes her head. "Thanks to these guys that someone will never touch me again." She plasters on a smile and continues to cook her food.

"Are you OK with that? Running from your problems instead of facing them head on?" I gently ask.

Capone's Chaos

"For now, yes. I needed time to heal and these guys have given me that. Even if I never become an Ol' Lady, I know my worth and what I enjoy. And I will never be shamed for it again." The strength in Rose's voice is noticeable. "I will never allow another person to destroy me that way again."

"Thank you." I place my palm on her shoulder, giving it a gentle squeeze.

"What are you thanking me for?" Rose asks, confused.

"For telling me a part of your story. I want to bury the past with you and this is a first step."

"Then, you're welcome." Rose turns the stove off. "Dinner is ready, enjoy." She walks away from the stove.

"Where are you going?" I ask.

"To my room so you all can eat." She looks at me with confusion in her eyes. Normally the patch whores don't eat with us, but I don't see her as a patch whore. I see her as a woman trying to make her way in a man's world.

I pull down a plate from the cupboard and hand it to her. "No, you're eating with us."

Her eyes ping to Red and he nods his head. "Are you sure?"

J. Lynn Lombard

"Positive. I want you to join us for dinner. No questions asked." I push the plate into Rose's hands and she takes it hesitantly.

"If you say so. But I'm not overstepping my role when Capone gets back." Rose fills her plate with the stir fry she made and the rest of us follow, sitting at the table and island.

"I'll make sure you don't have any issues when Capone gets back, Rose. I promise." I eat the delicious food she prepared and before I know it, I'm stuffed. "I can't eat anymore. That was excellent." I push my plate toward the center of the table.

Monica finishes her plate and together we stand. "We're heading to my room for the night," Monica announces. The prospect shoves the rest of his food down his throat, not even chewing. "You can stay here and finish your dinner, Prospect. We're inside the Clubhouse, safe and secure."

"I can't do that ma'am. Where you go, I go. Prez's orders." He says swallowing hard.

Monica glares at him and he washes his food down with his beer without even flinching. "Uh! Fine, but you're not coming into my room." She stomps out of the kitchen pulling me with her. The prospect hot on our heels. Monica spins around almost taking my arm out. "Look, I get you have a job to do, but back the fuck off. I don't need you breathing down my neck." He steps back a few feet, giving us breathing space.

Capone's Chaos

Monica opens the door to her and Blayze's room and shuts it in the prospect's face. She searches all over, for what I have no idea. She checks under the bed, in the closet, checks the latches on the windows and lastly checks the bathroom. Once she's satisfied with whatever she did or didn't find she sits on the bed and turns her T.V. on.

"What were you doing?" I ask.

"Making sure no one was in here." Monica shrugs her shoulders like it's no big deal.

"Why would there be someone in here?" I'm about to freak out thinking about all the worst possible scenarios when she answers me.

"It's a thing I do before I settle into a room. Since the attack, I have a compulsive disorder where I have to check every crack and crevice. To settle my mind that no one will jump out at me when I'm at my most vulnerable." Monica motions to the bathroom. "Go ahead and take your shower. I'll find something on T.V. and then we'll call Capone."

I grab my clothes and hurry into the bathroom. I take a shower, cleaning my body of the sweat I produced today during my work out. Thinking about what I'm going to tell Derek and how I'm going to tell him what Salazar has done. I also think about how I'll tell him I'm head over heels in love with him and want to spend the rest of my life by his side.

J. Lynn Lombard

Feeling clean and refreshed, I pull back the curtain and step out of the shower with a towel wrapped around my body. Monica's standing at the sink with tears streaming down her cheeks and her phone clutched tightly against her chest.

"Monica, what's wrong?" My mind plays the worst possible scenarios right now. Blayze is dead, someone kidnapped Aerial. Capone is hurt. "Monica," I snap my fingers in front of her face, pulling her from her daze.

"Get dressed, now. We have to go." She storms out of the room and begins stripping her clothes off. I follow her, sliding into my clothes.

"Monica, what the hell's going on?" I ask as I slip my shoes on. My wet hair is hanging down my back getting my shirt wet. A loud bang on her bedroom door startles me. Monica opens it and lets Red and Derange in.

"Let's go." Derange growls before walking back out of the room. He's pissed and agitated but no one's told me why. Red stands at the door, not saying a word, waiting for Monica and me. The flare of his nostrils tells me he's pissed too.

"Can someone tell me what the hell's going on?" I ask again.

Monica stops putting her hair up and turns toward me. "We need to go. I'll explain when we get there."

Capone's Chaos

"Get where? Monica, what the hell?" I grab her arm, turning her in my direction. Her eyes are red and puffy from crying. "Girl, you're scaring me. What is happening?"

"Blayze called." Monica pauses and takes a deep breath. "They were riding to Salazar's compound when a pickup came out of nowhere. He sideswiped Capone. I don't know how bad he's hurt."

"What?" I whisper. My heart sinks to my toes and my breathing becomes erratic. This is all my fault. If I only did what Salazar wanted, no one would be hurt. My mind starts playing out every worst case scenario in my head. He's bleeding out on the side of the road. He's paralyzed. He's dead and they're not telling me. I snap out of the dark thoughts plaguing my mind and snap into the present. Monica is watching me, waiting to see if I'll freak the fuck out or stay composed. "Let's go. Red, I'm riding with you. Monica can ride with Derange. Keep your prospects here to watch over the girls." I walk out of Monica's room with her and Red hot on my heels. We hurry to the garage where Derange is waiting. He has his helmet on already and hands Monica and me ours.

Monica slips hers on and I put mine on. Derange and Red are on their bikes, firing them up. I climb on behind Red and Monica gets on behind Derange. The guys peel out of the garage and the rolling gate is already opened by the time we reach it so we don't need to stop. The sun is setting against the horizon as we ride as fast as we can.

J. Lynn Lombard

I send up a prayer to the biker Gods and hope they're listening. I'm coming, Derek. Stay strong, stay with me.

Capone's Chaos

Chapter 11

Danyella

It took us a few hours to get here in El Bajio, Mexico, a little Mexican town south of Tijuana. It was the closest hospital from the accident. If this little building is what you'd call a hospital. The sun set a while ago, making it eerie as we pull down the quiet road. Homes are nestled side by side with thick fencing around each. The rumble of the bikes causes people sitting outside to stop what they're doing and watch.

Red and Derange park their bikes next to the other bikes sitting alongside the road. A man approaches us from the shadows and Red knuckle bumps him.

"They're inside waiting for you," the man says.

"Thanks, brother. Anything else?" Red asks.

"Nada. Quiet on the streets. I'm sure I'll turn something up by morning." I'm not sure who this man is but I'm guessing he's on our side. Which is a relief to know. "His bike will be fixed and out front by morning also."

"Thanks, man. Do what you can but stay safe." Red praises him.

"Si, Senor. We'll keep watch over your bikes while you're inside." He knuckle bumps Red and Derange and disappears into the shadows.

Red pops his kickstand down and settles the bike on it. He taps my leg and I hoist myself off and remove my helmet. Derange and Monica does the same. Before she's even completely off the bike, Blayze appears from behind the hospital and scoops her up into his arms, her helmet not even off her head. Monica wraps her arms around Blayze's neck and he pulls her against him, kissing her deeply. A deep pain laces my chest watching them and I hold my tears back.

Blayze breaks the kiss and rests his forehead against Monica's breathing her in. "Thank fuck you're OK. How's my brother?"

Blayze's eyes land on me and a sad smile crosses his face. He releases Monica and gives me a warm hug. I hold back the tears threatening to escape. Now isn't the time for a pity party. My man needs me to be strong for him and for his Club.

"Come on, I'll take you inside. He's doing OK, considering what happened." Blayze tucks Monica into his side and the five of us head inside. We walk

Capone's Chaos

around to the back of the building, under a blue tarp flapping in the breeze and turn left. The hospital just like the rest of the houses here is made of brick and mortar to keep them cool in the desert sun. From what I've learned in school, it's a cheap and effective way homes are built down here.

Blayze takes us up a set of stairs and turns left. The distinct beeping of monitors fills the narrow hallway. He leads us to a waiting room where Torch, Trigger, Dagger, Tiny and Bear are sitting or pacing back and forth. All eyes land on us when we walk into the room. The looks of sympathy are etched on each of their faces. It makes me want to break down, but I don't. I find strength in each of these men surrounding me to keep pushing forward.

"Have you heard anything yet?" I ask.

"Not yet. The Doc is in with him now." Torch's voice is gruff when he answers.

"What happened? How did this happen?"

"We were riding in formation to Salazar's compound when a pickup came out of nowhere and tried to take Capone out. He saw the pickup at the last second and swerved. Blayze laid his bike down to avoid hitting the pickup and Capone. Capone hit the box of the pickup with the side of his bike and went down, skidding across the gravel road. Before we could open fire, the driver took off. We haven't been able to find him yet." Torch retells what happened with vengeance in his voice.

J. Lynn Lombard

"And when we do find that motherfucker, I have something special planned for him," Blayze says, cracking his knuckles. The hatred in his voice sends a shiver down my spine. I forget these men are killers when it comes to taking care of people who hurt them or someone they care about. I chose not to see what they're capable of but hearing my brother talk about what he's going to do, it reminds me that they're not innocent by any means.

"Can I see him yet or the doctor?" I'm impatient to find Capone and know he's OK with my own eyes. They can tell me he's fine, but I need to see him for my own peace of mind.

"Yes, you can see him." A female voice says from behind me. I turn to find a beautiful woman standing in the doorway. She has long brown hair pulled up on top of her head and a white lab coat on. Her honey-colored eyes asses me and the rest of the men behind me. "I'm Dr. Perez." She extends her hand to me and I take it.

"Thank you, Dr. Perez. How's he doing?"

"He's stable. Capone has road rash from the fall where his leathers didn't protect him, some stitches in his head from where his helmet cut into it and bruised ribs from the handlebars on his bike. Follow me and I'll take you to him." Dr. Perez turns on her heels and walks out of the waiting room. Collective sighs release all around me. I hurry to keep up with the doctor, impatient to see Derek.

Capone's Chaos

"He's in here," she motions to the door. "I have him hooked up on monitors to keep track of his heart rate for the night. If he has a good rest, he'll be able to leave tomorrow sometime. Now, if you'll excuse me, I have some other things to do." Dr. Perez disappears out of sight, leaving me alone in front of Capone's closed door.

I inhale a deep breath and place my hand on the doorknob. Straightening my shoulders, I turn the knob and step into the room. Capone's laying on the bed, his eyes are closed. The monitor beeps softly in the small room. He has bandages around both arms and his head that I can see. He has tubes in his nose and an IV hooked up.

I quietly step into the room, so I don't disturb his sleep and sit in the chair next to Derek's bed. I take his hand in mine and it's cold to the touch. If it weren't for the monitors beeping, I'd think he wasn't sleeping. His tanned face is paler than normal. His larger than life form I'm used to seeing looks tired and sore laying here in the small bed. Derek squeezes my hand gently and turns his head in my direction. He opens his eyes and gives me a small smile.

"Danyella," he whispers.

"I'm here, Derek. I'm here." I squeeze his hand and he tries pulling me closer.

"Need to feel you next to me." He releases my hand and holds my cheek in the palm of his hand.

"You're hurt. I can't lay down with you." I shake my head.

"Yes, you can. I was scared I'd never get to see you again. Now get up here before I pull you onto this bed, injuring myself more." His voice is raspy and he wipes a tear from my cheek. "Don't cry, Belle. I'm fine, really. Just sore."

"I'm so relieved you're not hurt worse."

"So am I, now get over here." He pulls on my arm with strength I didn't think he had and I climb onto the bed, being careful of his injuries. Once I'm tucked into Derek's side, I lay my head on his chest, listening to his heartbeat, he relaxes. "That's better. Now get some sleep and we'll get out of here tomorrow."

"Derek," I pick my head up and look at his face. His chiseled jaw covered with a few days' old dark stubble, his perfect nose, his onyx eyes watching me. Even the bandage on his forehead, covering his black hair, Derek is my perfect man. The one I want to spend the rest of my life with, no matter what. "I love you. I've loved you for a long time. It just took my head a while to catch up to my heart."

"Belle." My heart skips a beat when he calls me that. Derek pulls me up so we're face to face. "I love you, too. No matter what, I want you by my side."

Capone's Chaos

"I'd like that." I place a soft kiss on his lips, savoring the warmth of his skin against mine. Capone grips the back of my head, holding me to him. A soft moan escapes his throat and he kisses me again. My body is on fire from his touch alone but I tamp it down. A hospital in Mexico while Derek is bandaged and sore, is not a place to have sex. I break the kiss and lay my head down next to Derek's. His heart monitor is beeping like crazy and I know if I put my hand against his chest, his heart would race under my touch.

Derek opens his eyes and the look of love and desire etched deep into the depth. "I'm happy you're here. Now I can sleep better with you next to me."

"Get some rest and we'll head out tomorrow." I carefully run my fingers over the top of his head where the bandage isn't covering his dark hair. He settles his head on my chest, his body against mine. I can feel his hard cock against the side of my hip. Stuffing the want and desire down, I settle into the bed with Derek and try to get some sleep. He needs it to recover and I need it from all the emotions I've been through today. Derek's soft snoring and warm body against mine lulls me into a deep sleep. The worry about Salazar and what he's trying to do slips from my mind with Derek next to me.

Sunlight streams through the windows and I stretch my arms over my head. My body is stiff from sleeping on this bed. Derek nuzzles his head between my breasts and it sets my body on fire with want.

"Good morning." Derek's voice is raspy from sleep, making him sound sexier than he normally does.

"Good morning. How are you feeling?" I run my hand through his dark hair, playing with the soft, silky strands.

"Better but stiff elsewhere if you keep doing that." He mumbles into my chest, vibrating my body. He pulls his head up, staring into my eyes, hypnotizing me. "I'm grateful I get this time with you again. I thought for sure that was the end yesterday."

"You have no idea how scared I was." I kiss him lightly on the lips. "What are we going to do now?"

"Now, I'm getting out of here and we're going to finish what we started before the accident." Derek carefully sits up, testing his muscles.

Now's the time I should tell him. I need to tell him, but fear holds me back. Fear of how he'll react. Fear of what he'll do when he finds out.

I can't live in fear anymore. I can't keep hiding from my problems and issues. I have to face them head on. I have to be strong. In order to be by Derek's side as his Ol' Lady, I need to tell him.

Capone's Chaos

"Derek," he stops getting dressed and turns to look at me. He has his jeans on but unbuttoned, no shirt and he looks sexy as hell even with bruised ribs and road rash. I inhale a deep breath. Time to rip the band-aid off. "Salazar is trying to blackmail me. He must have found out about how we felt for each other and now he's been trying to contact me. I've been ignoring his calls and texts, but I can't forever and I don't know what to do."

Derek's nostrils flare and his jaw ticks at a rapid pace. His sign he's pissed the fuck off. "How long has he been doing this and where's your phone?"

"About a week after you rescued me an unknown number popped up on my phone. I answered it without thinking who it could be and he told me if I didn't do what he wanted, he'd come after you and the club. I didn't say anything and after that, I ignored all calls and texts. My phone is full of unheard voicemails and unread text messages from him." I grab my phone I left on the stand turned off last night and hand it to him. "I don't know what to do and I have a feeling this is all my fault." Tears well up in my eyes as Derek takes my phone and powers it on. The dings of notifications come at us in rapid successions making my heart skip a beat. Shit, this is really bad.

"Who else knows about this?" Derek asks through clenched teeth.

J. Lynn Lombard

"I only told Monica about it yesterday before this happened. She doesn't know the extent of anything just that Salazar has contacted me."

"That means Blayze will know soon." He scrolls through my phone and the fury in his eyes is undeniable. Derek can usually remain composed and unaffected but this is something he can't control. "You didn't answer or read any of these?"

"Not a single one. Why what do they say?"

"Nothing you need to worry about right now. I'll take care of this. Can I keep your phone?" Derek looks me in the eyes. The fury is still there, but something else is too. Something he's promising without saying it.

"Yes, you can keep it. I don't want anything to do with it." Derek pockets my phone and offers me his hand. I grab onto it like a lifeline.

"I will keep you safe but we can't have any more secrets. Is there anything else I need to know about?" Derek rubs his thumbs along my knuckles soothing me.

"That's it. Nothing else." I shake my head. "Where does this leave us?" I ask the question I've been afraid to know the answer too.

"This changes nothing between us. You're mine and I won't let anyone hurt you again." Derek pulls me against his warm, naked chest and I wrap my arms around him, grateful he isn't tossing me aside.

Capone's Chaos

"I'm so sorry for not telling you or anyone sooner. I was afraid, Derek." He runs his hands down my back in soothing motions.

"I get it, but in order for me to protect you, there can't be anything else between us. I can't protect what I don't know about." Derek cups my chin so I'm looking into his dark eyes. "You are mine." He kisses me hard. I open my mouth allowing him entrance and his tongue plunges inside. We battle back and forth with so much passion and chaos, I'm breathless and dizzy by the time we pull apart. I whimper, missing his mouth on mine and Derek gives me another soft kiss.

"Let's get out of here. I need to fill the Club in on what happened." He tries to put his shirt on, but grunts in pain. I stand up and take his shirt from his hands. I help him pull it over his head and he tugs it down. "That sucked. I'll be fine in a few." Derek is winded from putting his shirt on, but I have a feeling no matter how bad he's hurt, nothing will stop him from going after Salazar.

Once he's dressed, he offers me his hand and together we leave his hospital room. We go into the waiting area that's full of all his brothers, his club, his family. No one left last night. A look of relief passes across all their faces when they see Derek. Monica approaches him and hugs him hard, making Derek wince in pain.

"I'm fine, Monica. Thank you." Monica releases Derek and touches the bandage on his head. He removes it and reveals a line of perfect stitches starting at the top where his ear connects to his head, across his temple, leading into his hairline.

"Prez, that's going to be gnarly." Trigger admires Derek's stitching. It's puffy and red but it doesn't change how I feel about him.

"Thanks? I think." Derek shakes his head. "We need a secure place to stay for a few days where the girls will be safe. We have business to finish down here with Salazar and it'll be tricky to take them back home and come back undetected. Any word on who that was that tried to hit me?"

Blayze speaks up, "I have a trusted friend of the Club down here. He's arranged a place for us to stay and has his ear to the ground trying to find out who that was. We should know something soon."

"Then let's get the fuck out of here and regroup where it's secure. We have a lot to discuss." Derek wraps his arm around my shoulder and we leave the hospital with the rest of the Royal Bastards behind us.

It's still early in the morning but the humidity is unbearable. Derek and I walk under the blue tent flapping in the light breeze and around the corner that leads to the street. The same man who spoke to Red and Derange approaches us. He looks tired but offers his hand to Derek and then Blayze.

Capone's Chaos

"Thanks for being on watch last night. It's appreciated and you have the protection of our club." Derek offers the man.

"Thank you." He looks around before handing Derek a piece of paper. "There's an address to a safe house down here and the name of the man you're looking for. When you end these assholes, I'll be able to rest easier."

"Thanks, man." Derek takes the paper and puts it in the inside pocket of his cut.

"One more thing you need to know before I disappear." The man looks around again before continuing. "I found Layla. Well, technically I found info about Layla. You're not going to like it. All the info you need is at the safe house. I know you said you didn't care what happened to her, but you need to know."

My shoulders stiffen at the mention of her name but I try not to show any reaction. Derek squeezes my shoulders in an attempt to reassure me.

"I didn't ask for anything on her. She's a part of my past I want to keep buried." Derek's voice is gruff with anger.

"I know you didn't ask about her, but you need to know. It's all there when you're ready." The man leads us to where the bikes are parked. Derek sees his and his jaw drops.

"I'll forgive you for that because she's fixed." He releases me and walks over to his bike, looking it over. "How'd you get it fixed so fast?"

"I know a guy." He shrugs his shoulders. "Listen, I want to apologize for what my sister did. She was in a bad place at the time and didn't know any other way out."

Derek rises from admiring his fixed bike, his jaw ticking. "What the fuck are you talking about? What did Layla do?"

"It's all at the safe house. That's all I can say out loud. All I can do is apologize in advance for it." The man, now knowns as the bitch's brother disappears before anyone can say anything.

"Load up and roll out," Derek commands before straddling his bike. He puts on a new helmet and motions for me to climb on the back. I hesitate, my insecurities are ramping up inside my head at the mention of Layla and Derek sees it. He climbs off his bike and pulls me into his chest. "I didn't ask to know anything about her. I swear I don't want to know." Derek tries to soothe the mess of my emotions.

"I believe you, but now what do we do? What if she is there and you find out you want her and not me anymore? What if I'm just a passerby and you're really in love with her? What if all this is my fault because I pushed you away so many times when we were younger?" Word vomit comes flowing out of my mouth before I can stop it.

Capone's Chaos

"Hey," Derek lifts my face to meet his eyes. There's love and tenderness in them even after my outburst. "There is nothing she can give or ever gave me that you didn't. Honestly, even when we did things, you're all I could think about. Anytime I touched her, I imagined it was you. Which might sound weird, but she is in the past. Everything I ever did with her is in the past where it needs to stay buried. She wasn't you. She will never be you. You are the one I've always wanted and craved. Not a barmaid. Not anyone else. Just you. You are mine, just as I am yours."

Derek leans in and kisses me like no other to seal his words. Everything he just said he pours out into our heated kiss. He's mine. Derek, aka Capone, Combs belongs to me, just like I belong to him.

My ride or die. My other half. We're in this together and whatever surprise this bitch has done, we will face it head on together.

J. Lynn Lombard

Chapter 12

Capone

The look of insecurities that crossed my Belle's face broke my heart. I had to reassure her there is nothing I want from Layla. Danyella doesn't understand how long or far my infatuation with her went so I had to prove it. Not only with my words but with my actions too. So, after I confessed to her the truth of my time with Layla, I gave her the most passionate kiss we've ever shared. Where our souls connect on another level. Danyella is mine and I am hers. I've always belonged to her, I was just an idiot who needed to scratch an itch to pass the time. Now I hope that decision doesn't bite me in the ass.

After releasing Danyella from my grasp, I gaze into her green eyes. She's speechless and breathless. The heaving of her chest does things to my heart.

"What was that for?" Danyella whispers.

"To show you no matter what, you're mine," I growl.

Capone's Chaos

"You mean, you're mine." She giggles. The tension in the air dissipates with her laughter.

"Yeah, that too," I smirk and brush a strand of hair out of her face.

"If you two are about done sucking face, I'd like to get out of this heat soon." Bear's boisterous voice echoes around us. Blayze grumbles something about keeping my tongue out of his sister's mouth and Monica smacks him with a grin on her face.

I release Danyella from my grasp and straddle my bike. She slides on behind me and settles against my back. It's thrilling having her on my bike this way, her tits and thighs plastered against me. Last time she was on it, she didn't want to be and kept far away as possible. Which was hard, but she barely managed to hang onto me. This time though, this time her hands are around my waist, dangerously low and her warmth is against my back.

I pull the paper Ricardo gave me from my cut and study the address. I know of the area and it'll be tricky getting there, but we can do it. It's about a forty-minute ride to the middle of nowhere Mexico. A safe house nestled in the middle of a small-town full of shanties. The best place to stay, in plain sight.

The rumble of our bikes sets my soul free. The vibration of my Harley underneath me and my Belle tucked behind me makes me feel like everything is set right in the world. Belle is where she's always destined to be, on the seat of my bike, her legs spread wide with me between them. During the whole ride, her hands keep brushing my stomach and dick, making me hard riding down the dirt roads. At one point, I leaned back and her fingers dove inside my jeans, stroking my cock. I almost crashed again her hands felt so good wrapped around my shaft. She stops just before I explode in my jeans and a growl rips from my throat, warning her she better be ready for me when we get there.

Danyella breathes on the side of my neck, staying as close to me as possible, sending want and lust roaring through my body. She's going to get a good fucking as soon as we get there. Thirty minutes later, I pull into a little village with shanties nestled so close to each other, there's no breathing room. I follow the directions to a small warehouse hidden inside the village. Which is good because we can pull our bikes in and not have them spotted from the street.

I stop my bike and put the kickstand down.

"Stay here," I tell Danyella and Monica and motion for Blayze and Torch to follow me. The three of us walk up to the barn style doors and push them open. We enter the warehouse and check each and every room before allowing the girls in. I'm in the kitchen searching when an envelope with my name scrawled across the front catches my attention on the counter. I pick it up and stuff it into the inside pocket of my cut. Not sure if I want to read it or leave it be. That's something I'll talk with Danyella about. If I do, I want to do it with her.

"All clear," Blayze's voice echoes in the empty room. I hurry from the kitchen, go outside and pull my bike inside with the rest of the Royal Bastards following me. Our bikes fill the warehouse floor, cutting the echoing down substantially. I tap Danyella on the leg and she climbs off from behind me. I put my kickstand down and get off too.

"We have some shit to go over and a plan to put into place. Everyone meet in the kitchen in ten." I order before taking Danyella's hand and explore the safe house with her. We climb up a set of metal stairs and when we reach the top, I turn. The mezzanine overlooks the entire warehouse from up here. There isn't a place I can't see from this vantage point. Danyella opens one bedroom door and steps inside. I follow close behind and shut the door behind me. Pulling her against me, I kiss her with pent up passion from the ride over. By the time I release her lips, Danyella is panting heavily, her eyes are half lidded and full of desire.

"You're a fucking tease. You know that right," I growl into the side of her neck, nibbling and kissing her succulent skin. Danyella moans from my touch.

"Just giving you a taste of what you do to me daily," she whispers. I pick her up so her legs are wrapped around my waist. I can feel the heat from her pussy rubbing against my aching cock. Wanting to sink deep inside of her but knowing we can't right now. I kiss the curve of Danyella's neck again and release her, letting her body slide down mine until her feet touch the floor. Her cheeks are rosy and she looks at me through hooded eyes.

"We have to head back downstairs. I think this room will do." Danyella taps me on the chest, kisses me and saunters out of the bedroom. She sways her hips back and forth teasing the ever loving fuck out of me.

"Woman, if you don't put that pop away, I'm going to say fuck heading back downstairs and tie you up to that bed post," I growl low in my throat. Danyella turns around. Her eyes start at my toes and trail up my entire body all while she's biting her bottom lip.

"Promises, promises, Capone. You won't do that because even I know the rules. Club comes first. So let's get this meeting over with so you can deliver on that promise." With that Danyella disappears down the iron stairs and heads into the kitchen. I rub my hand over my chest to slow my racing heart. This woman will be the death of me if I can't get myself under control. All she has to do is be on my mind and I'm ready to sink balls deep into her.

Danyella sticks her head out the kitchen door and shouts up at me, "Capone, are you coming?" Then My Belle has the fucking nerve to laugh. She fucking cackles when she heads back into the kitchen.

Capone's Chaos

Shaking my head, I stomp down the stairs and across the concrete floor. I'm going to blister her ass red for pulling that stunt. But I can't be too mad because even though she called me out, my dick is rock hard behind the zipper of my jeans. I slam my hand against the swinging door leading into the kitchen and glare at Danyella. She's staring right back at me, daring me to say something. The fire in her eyes and the teasing smile on her face is my undoing. I walk over to her and lean over her sitting in the chair. My arms are caging her in.

"Do that again and see what happens, My Belle," I whisper low, my mouth right next to her ear.

Danyella shivers against my threat. She turns her head so we're nose to nose. "I'm counting on it, Capone." A rumble starts low in my throat when someone clears theirs behind me.

"If you're done, we need to get down to business." Blayze stomps into the kitchen and plops down in another chair. He pulls Monica onto his lap. The rest of the Royal Bastards walks into the kitchen. The room is intense as they all wait for me to begin. Danyella stands up and offers me her seat. I sit down and pull her onto my lap. These next few things require her presence so she stays.

"I've come across some important information this morning and we need to move fast on it. Apparently, I'm not the only one Salazar has targeted. He tried hitting us where it hurts and that's with Danyella."

Blayze's body stiffens and his head turns slowly in our direction. "What?"

"He tried contacting me a week after I was rescued. I've been ignoring his calls and texts this whole time, but the last one he sent me." Danyella pauses and catches her breath. "This last one was a few hours before Capone's accident. He said our time is up and if I don't meet him, he'll kill Capone."

"Danyella, you didn't tell me that," Monica hisses.

"Capone was safe, so I didn't feel I needed too." Danyella defends herself.

"Well, if you did, he wouldn't be hurt. Are you fucking kidding me? We don't hide secrets in this club. Not after what happened in Detroit." Monica glares at Danyella, crossing her arms over her chest.

"How the hell am I supposed to know what's going on? I've been an outcast here since I came back!" Danyella's tears are running down her face and her voice has an angry edge to it. "You all have been treating me like I'm some piece of fucking glass that'll break if the wrong thing is said or done. And I'll tell you all, that's far from the truth. I'm not some scared little girl who can't handle the truth so stop treating me like a child! Then maybe, just maybe I would have come to you sooner!" Danyella slams her fists on the table, shoving her point home.

"Are we done now?" I ask. My jaw ticks with each passing second.

"I am," Danyella's voice is soft in the large room.

"So am I," Monica grumbles.

"Good. Now, here's how we're going to handle this. Danyella, you're going to text Salazar and set up a meeting. Tell him how you know it was him who hit me. That you don't know the condition I'm in because the rest of the Club doesn't trust you. When he sets up the meeting place, we'll be there and take him out once and for all."

"What if he doesn't believe me?"

"Make him believe you. This is our shot at taking back our control and ending this motherfucker." I gently nudge Danyella, handing her phone to her. She sighs and sets her phone on the table. Taking a deep breath, My Belle finds the courage to do this. She picks up her phone and an image I've never seen before stares back at me. It's a picture of me on my Harley wearing my leathers and my sunglasses on. The sun is setting in the background, making the sky light up red and pink. It's a really good picture of me.

"When did you take this?" I question, pulling the phone out of her hand.

J. Lynn Lombard

"Uh... the day we came back from Michigan. You were sitting outside on your bike, thinking about something and I loved the way you looked. So I snuck a picture." Danyella's cheeks turn fire engine red with embarrassment.

Remembering that day, a smile graces my lips. "I was thinking about how I was going to win you over. That's ironic." I hand Danyella back her phone. "Go ahead and send the text."

She opens her text apps and begins typing. It takes a while for her to find the right words, but when she's satisfied with it, she hits send. "There. Now we wait and see if he bites."

No sooner the words leave her lips, Danyella's phone lights up with an incoming call. It's an unavailable number. I nudge her to answer it on speakerphone and shush the rest of the guys.

"Hello?" Danyella whispers into the phone.

"Danyella, Danyella, Danyella. What a pleasant surprise. I didn't think I'd hear from you after all this time." Salazar's gravely voice comes across the line. It takes every ounce of willpower I have not to reach through the phone and rip out his tongue and then beat him with it.

"Well, I got your point loud and clear. Did you want to kill him?" Her voice shakes with fear. She's playing the part very well.

Capone's Chaos

"My Belle. That's what he calls you isn't it?" The nickname I gave Danyella rolls past Salazar's lips in a taunting tone. "You know better than that. Of course I didn't want to kill Capone, I want you anyways and this way brought you out of hiding. Why don't you tell me where you are and I'll come and get you."

"That's not how it works, Salazar. I'll come to you. Obviously, you either take what you want or have them murdered and I'd rather take my chances finding my way to you than you come to me." The hatred in Danyella's voice is unmistakable and it's turning me on.

"Fine, I'll be at the bar in six hours. Ask your brother where it is, he's been there before and just recently too. You have until then to make it there. If you don't you can kiss your precious Derek goodbye for good. I might even throw in a two-fer. Derek and Xander." He hangs up on Danyella before she can rebut and she sets the phone down.

"There, now we need to make a plan on how we keep everyone safe in the time limit we have." Danyella stands up from my lap, "I need a minute." With that, she's out of the kitchen taking the time she needs. It's been a whirlwind of emotions for her and I have one more the two of us need to discuss.

"What's the plan, Prez?" Red asks.

"Pull up the details on the bar and the safehouse. Why does Salazar want to meet there and

J. Lynn Lombard

what's so special about that shitty place? Monica will drive Danyella there. Red, Tiny, Trigger and Torch, you four will be there already watching the place. Blayze, Derange, Dagger and I will follow Danyella to the bar to make sure she gets there safely. Then when she finds out what he wants, we get Danyella out of there and set fireworks to the fucking place. Leaving no one inside to survive." I slam my fists on the table, making it rattle with force. "Are we in agreement? Say, aye." All my brothers say aye, every single one of them has mine and my girls back. "Anyone in disagreement, say nay." Silence descends upon the room.

"Good," I slam my fist on the table again, ending the meeting. "Now get ready to load up and roll out. I want you four there like now, not later."

"Aye, Prez." Torch nods his head. "We will protect Danyella and Monica with our lives." He holds his pointer finger and middle finger on his left hand up in a peace sign and places it over his heart. I return the gesture and four of them leave the kitchen. Torch is a strange fucker and he has his quirks, but whatever helps him to get the job done, I'll support.

Monica, Blayze, Derange and Dagger all disperse into different areas of the safehouse. Each doing their own thing to be prepared for tonight. Which leaves me sitting in the kitchen alone. I pull the letter out of my cut and flip it over, trying to figure out if I want to open it or leave the past to rest.

Capone's Chaos

Chapter 13

Danyella

The lost look on Derek's face when I enter the room is my undoing. Something is bothering him and I don't know what it is. He's holding an envelope in his hands, a slight tick in his jaw. I approach him and he shoves the envelope back into his cut. His hands roam my legs, caressing my thighs. Whatever he was contemplating disappears the moment his lips fall upon mine.

Derek's hot breath on my chest sends a shot of desire through my body. I want this man more than words can express. More than actions can attest. He is my soul, my heart and a part of me. I pull his face back up to mine and kiss him hard. My tongue battles with his until we're both breathing hard. I rise and yank my shirt over my head, exposing my chest to him. Derek licks his lips and watches me. He adjusts his cock and spreads his legs wide. With wild abandonment, knowing we could be caught at any time, I unhook my bra and toss it in his direction. Next, I shimmy my jeans down my hips and kick them off so I'm left in only my panties.

J. Lynn Lombard

Derek slides his cut off and places it on the table. Then he chucks his shirt off, making my mouth water. Now he's in just his jeans, the zipper and button undone, revealing the sexy V most men work hard to achieve. He motions to me with one finger and I strut over to him, swaying my hips. He pulls me against him and kisses my neck. I arch my back to his touch and let our bodies speak to each other. I moan when his lips descend onto my nipple, sucking and nipping.

"I need you, Derek." He picks me up so I wrap my legs around his waist. He places me onto the table, the cold metal nipping at my skin. His hand descends down my body into my panties. Derek plays with my clit driving me wild with need.

"You're so wet for me, Belle. This is going to be fast. Then later I can cherish your body the way you deserve." I hear the clink of his belt as he drops his jeans to his ankles. Derek pulls me to the edge of the table so my ass is hanging off it. He runs his cock up and down my wet folds, teasing me. Before words can leave my mouth, Derek drives into me and fills me with his cock. He pumps in and out, hard and fast. His strokes leave a fire stoked in my soul. We're bare skin against bare skin. Our hearts pumping hard against each beat. "If anyone deserves to have my child, it should be you, Belle."

I'm not sure where that came from but holy shit, I don't question it. Not with the way Derek fucks me like he never wants to let me go. He ravishes my body with his own until I'm a withering mess beneath him. His long, hard strokes sends my body into a tailspin of chaos and need. His lips find mine and he kisses me hard as I fall over the edge, taking him with me.

Once he slows down and I'm sated, Derek rests his forehead against mine. "You are mine, Belle."

I hold his face in the palms of my hands, "You are mine, Derek."

"Forever." He pulls out of me and I immediately miss his body against mine. "I need you to promise me you'll be safe when meeting Salazar. I can't lose you."

I slide my panties on along with my jeans, just in case anyone walks in. I approach Derek, "I will. I won't let him hurt me, you or anyone else anymore."

Derek kisses me again and pulls away. "I'll be with you every step of the way."

"I know." He hands me my shirt and I slide it on. I can still feel his come between my legs. "You know we didn't use anything."

"I know. Like I said, if anyone deserves my child, it's you, Belle. I'm an asshole and go after what I want. What I want right now is your belly swollen with my child."

J. Lynn Lombard

A smile graces my lips and I kiss Derek again. No more words are needed with where we stand. We are together forever and if I do end up pregnant, then that's God's way of tying us together even further.

***

It's dark by the time Monica and I leave the safehouse. We're driving a black Dodge Ram Derek was able to get from Ricardo. How he can get these things under the Cartel's radar is a question I don't want an answer too.

Now, we need to focus on Salazar and end his terror on us. Monica pulls into a deserted parking lot that is near a rundown bar. There are a couple of pickups parked haphazardly and a sleek black SUV next to the doors. I don't see any of the Royal Bastards around, but I know they're here. Monica puts the truck in park and looks over to me.

"When we go in there, please be careful. Don't get to close to Salazar where he can grab you and use you for a shield. Once we know he's in there, get the hell out and Torch will light the place up like the fourth of July." She squeezes my shoulder. "I'll be waiting right out these doors for you."

"Why don't we light it up now?" I question. If they think it'll be that simple, then just torch it now, not wait.

Capone's Chaos

"Because we need to know for sure he's in there. Keep your phone on and Derek has his muted. So he can hear everything but they can't hear him." Monica dials Derek from my phone and flashes it to me. She hands it to me and I shove it in my jeans pocket.

Together we open our door and close them, making our way up the stairs to the bar. She squeezes my shoulder in encouragement and I walk through the doors, alone. Monica staying on the front porch watching for anyone trying to sneak up on us. The first thing that I see is four men gathered around a booth. Once the door shuts behind me, they all turn in my direction. Dust and dirt are caked on every surface beside the booth. I take a hesitant step away from the door when a large hand lands on my shoulder, making me jump. I junk punch the guy and he goes down like a sack of bricks.

"Now is that any way to treat my guest?" The man sitting at the booth asks the man on the ground holding his balls. "Come, Danyella. Join me for a drink, no?" He opens a bottle of scotch and pours two glasses. I look over my shoulder and see another man blocking the door.

"Why is there a man blocking the door?" I ask loud enough for Derek on the other line to hear. So he knows I can't get out.

"Please, join me. It's rude to not drink when offered." The intent in Salazar's voice is unmistakable. If I don't go there, he will kill me on the spot. I take a small step toward him when shots ring out through the bar. I duck and crawl behind the bar's counter. Bullets rain down onto me and splinter into the wood above my head. I lift my head to see if I can find an escape route when a small whimper catches my attention. I head to the middle of the counter and look inside a small hiding spot. A little girl stares back at me with tears in her eyes and her lips are trembling. She has a pert nose and wide-set black eyes. Her features look familiar to me but I can't place where I've seen her before.

With renewed strength, I gather the little girl in my arms and hurry toward the stock room in the back of the bar. Bullets whiz past my head and splinter into the wood, sending shards in my direction. The little girl doesn't scream but she does bury her head into my chest, hiding her face.

I cover her body with mine the best I can and slam the door shut. I look around and see there's no back door. Shit. The sound of bullets stops for a moment and the smell of copper and gun powder is thick in this room. Looking up I spy a small slider window covered with dirt and sand. I grab some boxes with the little girl still clinging to me and stack them up against the wall.

"Hang on, baby girl. I'm going to get us out of here and we'll find my friends." I soothe her. She nods her head, her body trembling with sobs. "Can you tell me your name?" She doesn't answer me.

Capone's Chaos

Instead of wasting time, I grab more boxes and stack them higher so we can reach the window.

I set the little girl on her feet, but she doesn't let go of my neck. "Listen, I need you to climb these boxes and out the window. I'll be right behind you. Can you do that for me? Can you be a big girl and get out that window?" I point to the window waiting for her to answer.

A loud bang comes from the door and my heart races in my chest. They're coming for us and we don't have much time. "Please, baby girl. I need you to climb to safety." I plead.

The little girl hesitantly releases my neck and begins climbing up. The banging on the door increases and it shudders with every slam. I quickly throw things in front of it to prevent it from opening. I turn around to see how she's doing and she's almost to the top.

"That's it. You're doing great, honey. Just a little further." I encourage her. She continues to climb until she's at the window. Looking down at me with uncertainty, I make the decision to climb up behind her. These boxes won't hold our weight for too long. Once I reach the top, I pop open the window and sit on the sill. It's a drop down but we need to do it.

"Climb into my back and don't let go. I'm going to get us down from here. Can you do that?" She nods her head with fear in her black eyes. Once she's secure, I turn so my stomach is against the windowsill and my feet are dangling. The door to the supply room bursts open and I come face to face with the man I junk punched pointing a gun right at my head. I send up a prayer that we make the drop and release my hold on the windowsill just as a bullet flies at my head. My feet are dangling in the air. I don't know how far I have to drop, but I have to do it before he catches me.

I release my hold and we fall to the ground, my body taking the brunt of the fall. I land on my front side, keeping her protected. The impact jars my feet all the way up to my stomach. I feel sick but know we need to keep moving. I pick myself up off the ground and help the little girl up. She clings to me so I pick her up and we start running in the direction away from the bar.

A light shining far off in the distance is my goal. My body aches, my head is pounding and my stomach is queasy but I can't stop for anything. The light gets brighter and brighter the closer we get. I spot a shiny black Harley and relief fills my body. I collapse right before voices reach me. My body drifts into a dark, voided place.

Capone's Chaos

Epilogue

Capone

It's been a few hours since we came back from the biggest fucking set up ever done. I failed my Belle and now she's hurt because of me. Red and Derange have her in the room she picked out back at the safehouse. Derange said she wasn't hurt, but fuck, the way she collapsed right before she reached me, I thought she was dead. And the little girl she had with her? I have no idea who she is or what she's doing here. But that will be back seated for now. Now my top priority is Danyella.

After Danyella's phone cut out the moment she stepped into the bar, I knew it was a setup. We tried to manhandle the door and that's when the shots were fired from inside. After that, I didn't hold back. I went in guns blazing and took down the main heads of the Salazar Cartel. Including Salazar himself. Then when Danyella came running from around the building, directly toward me, I sent Torch to do his magic. He lit that motherfucking place up like the fourth of July on crack.

J. Lynn Lombard

The letter written to me is sitting on the table. My head is resting on my hands when the kitchen door swings open. Danyella comes into the kitchen and spots me sitting here. It's now or never. I shove out a seat, motioning her to sit next to me. She slowly makes her way over with her eyebrows drawn together and her lips pursed. I appraise the most beautiful woman I've ever had the pleasure of knowing. From her feet to the tips of her hair, Danyella is absolutely perfect to me and for me.

"What's that?" She asks, motioning to the envelope in my hand.

I place it on the table between us, my name scrawled on the front facing both of us. "This was here when I got here. I haven't opened it yet and I wanted to make this decision with you. Do we want to leave whatever's in this letter unread or do we want to do it together?"

Danyella picks up the envelope and looks it over. Then her green eyes land on me full of understanding and love. "What do you want to do?"

I fold my fingers in front of my face with my elbows on the table, like a prayer. "I don't know." I point to the letter. "What I do know is that can't be any good."

"But you'll drive yourself crazy if you don't read it." Danyella nails the issue on the head. She's exactly right. If that letter answers anything about what happened five years ago, I'll want to know.

Capone's Chaos

Danyella's thumb slides under the seal and rips it open. She pulls out a piece of paper and a picture floats between us onto the table. It's a photo of a little girl with jet black hair and dark eyes, like my own. Her features are similar to mine but there's no fucking way this can be. I pick the picture up and study it. Her pert little nose is scrunched and she isn't smiling the way a child should be.

"What the fuck?" I question and look up at Danyella. She's reading the letter with tears pooling in her eyes, making them a dark green. She hasn't seen the picture yet and the image is the same little girl Danyella saved a few hours ago.

"Capone," Danyella starts reading the letter. "I know this isn't what you wanted and I know this isn't your fault. You didn't know what Salazar had planned when he learned where his grandson was. He hired me to trick you into sleeping with me and I did it. I'm no better than he is, but this little girl doesn't deserve the outcome Salazar had planned for her. I was a pawn in his game and had no choice but to follow through with what he wanted. When I found out I was pregnant, Salazar wanted to use my little girl to lure you out. Only he didn't expect me to fight back. I spent the last six years keeping her safe, away from Salazar.

"If you're finding this letter, it means Salazar found me and I'm no longer breathing. I did something he never would have dreamed I could do. To him, I was the hired hand who went with everything he said and wanted. But the moment I felt that first kick, to the first time I heard her heartbeat, I knew I'd sacrifice my life to save hers.

"I wanted to do this face to face, but I had no way of getting her to you safely. I enclosed a picture of my little girl, Nina. Our little girl. Please, take care of her and protect her the way she deserves. My brother, Ricardo, knows how to find Nina and when you're ready, he will bring her to you. Please forgive me for deceiving you all these years and don't take it out on her. She's an innocent brought into this cruel, harsh world. I have told her who her daddy is and she's anxious to meet you. Layla."

I take the letter from Danyella's hands and read it over. It's written right here in black pen. I have a little girl I had no idea about. Anger radiates through my body from missing her first cries, her first steps, her first words. Missing all the milestones and goals Nina has taken.

"Derek," Danyella whispers. "What are you going to do?" The look of hurt and betrayal crosses her beautiful face.

"I don't know. All I know is this woman could be lying to get me to take a kid that isn't mine. After everything I've witnessed and seen, every lie in my past, this could be the exact same thing." I clench the letter in my grip until it crinkles.

Danyella picks up the photo and studies it. The moment realization crosses her face, I see it. The look of determination and unbridled passion. "I don't think she's lying to you. If this little girl is yours, we are going to raise her and take care of her. We will do this together."

"Are you sure? I would never ask you to raise another woman's child."

Danyella stands up from her chair and approaches me. Her body is still sore from her escape from death, but that doesn't stop her. She straddles my lap so we're chest to chest. She grips my face in the palm of her hands, forcing me to look at her. "If this little girl is a part of you, I have no problem loving her like she's my own. Even if she isn't yours, I have no problem taking care of an innocent little girl who has so much to give. But by the looks of her and you, I wouldn't doubt she is yours. Even if you can't see it."

I wrap my arms around Danyella's waist and hold her tight. "I don't know what I'd do without you, Belle. You're the light in my dark world."

"Right now, you can kiss me and then we can go wherever it may lead." And I do, I kiss Danyella with so much passion, I'm dizzy and breathing heavily. Her pussy grinds into my cock, making it hard behind the zipper of my jeans. I kiss my way down her throat to her heaving chest. Danyella throws her head back, bringing her plump tits up to my face. "Together, Derek. We'll conquer this together."

J. Lynn Lombard

      Even in all the chaos of the Club life and our lives, we will do it together.

Capone's Chaos

Note from the Author:

First off, I want to start with my wonderful readers. Thank you for taking the time to read this book. I hope you're enjoying the Royal Bastards MC world.

Crimson and Nikki, thank you for letting me be a part of this world and trusting me to do it right. Without the support behind all the authors in this world, Blayze never would've come to life. So, thank you again for allowing me to be a part of this world.

My Beta Bitches! Joy, Monica, Krista and Sherry. Finding my mistakes and pumping me up for this release. You ladies are my girls and always will be. Thank you for your late-night messages and for letting me be a part of your lives. You're forever in mine. Sarah, my Ride or Die. You've been with me since Racing Dirty (even before that with the novels in the vault) Thank you for your editing and feedback on all my work. Without you, I would have never pushed that publish button.

Kat, thank you so much for jumping in and proofreading this novel for me. Your feedback was amazing and you did it with a small timeline. Thank you so much for the extra set of eyes! I'm forever indebted to you.

Michelle, oh where to start? We've been together since before Indy publishing (Kind of forced since you're my sister in law) but I wouldn't have it any other way. You're stuck with me for life. Oh! And

J. Lynn Lombard

AARP called, they're still waiting for you to fill out that paperwork.

Rex and my spawns. Each book is written is for you. Thank you for putting up with my ass on a daily basis. I love you all from the bottom of my heart.

Lastly, I want to thank my dad. If it wasn't for your love of reading, I never would have pursued doing this. Thank you for your support and undying love of the written word.

Capone's Chaos

Books written by J. Lynn Lombard

Royal Bastards MC

Blayze's Inferno

Capone's Chaos

Savage Saints MC

Kayne's Fury

Blayde's Betrayal

Stryker's Salvation

All are #FreeonKU

Find the stories that started all of this in the completed **Racing Dirty Series**

Thrust

Torque (book 2)

Turbulence (book 3) Amazon

Call my Bluff Anthology

J. Lynn Lombard

Want to keep in touch with me?

Join my mailing list at http://bit.ly/2u71A8P

Join J. Lynn's Badass Bitches reader group on Facebook: http://bit.ly/2qtxkpw

Follow me on Amazon: http://amzn.to/2COi78o

Goodreads: http://bit.ly/2CP2fCH

Bookbub: http://bit.ly/2HkczDZ

Instagram: www.instagram.com/j.lynnlombardauthor

Printed in Great Britain
by Amazon